Diary of a Horse Mad Girl

The Full Collection

Books 1 to 5

By Katrina Kahler

Copyright © KC Global Enterprises

Table of Contents

Book 1

My First Pony

Dedication

This book is dedicated to my beautiful daughter. These are her adventures and we all loved going along for the ride. I hope you do too!

Hi, my name is Abbie and this diary is all about me and my very first pony, Sparkle who is a beautiful 13 hand Palomino. She is the best first pony anyone could wish for and we've had so many great adventures together. Luckily, I live on a rural property with lots of land and also other neighborhood girls to ride with. We have our very own "Saddle Club" and it's such a great way to grow up. I have many fun times to share with you and if you're anywhere near as horse mad as me, I'm sure you'll enjoy reading this book.

Now, from the beginning...

Monday 24 September

When I heard Sparkle nicker this morning, I knew she was calling me. I raced over to the paddock still in my PJs. I couldn't get there quickly enough! I can't believe I now actually have my own pony! And she's such a beautiful palomino. They've always been my favorite type of horse and now I have one of my very own. It's like a dream come true. One minute, I'm being led around the paddock on my neighbor's horse and the next minute I'm standing there with my own palomino.

I'm lucky as well, to have a girl like Ali as my neighbor. She's really nice to me and also a great rider. If it wasn't for her living next door with horses of her own, this probably wouldn't be happening. She and her mum know everything there is to know about horses, which is such a great help, because my parents don't know much at all. And now that I have my own pony to ride, we can go riding together. It's great having an older girl next door who is as horse mad as me. I always wanted a big sister. I'm very lucky!

And guess what! Sparkle loves bananas. Who would ever have thought that horses would eat bananas – with the skin and all! I'm going to give her one every day as a special treat. I'll have to make sure Mom buys lots of carrots as well.

I'm so glad it's the school holidays and I can spend every day with her. My new grooming kit is really cool too – it's in a special pink box and everything in it is pink. And the best part is…Sparkle loves being brushed. She's such a good pony and Ali says I'm very lucky to have found a pony with a quiet temperament like hers.

I can't wait for my first riding lesson on Thursday. The instructor is coming at 9:00 in the morning before it gets hot, so I'll have to be up early to make sure I'm ready. I don't think I'll be able to sleep tonight, just thinking about it! I'm so excited!!!

Ali and her first pony

Thursday 27 September

I thought that the day Sparkle arrived at our place was the best day of my life, but I think today was even better. That riding lesson was so awesome and Jane, the instructor, says I'm a natural. She said I have a really good seat and Mom was commenting on my posture and how straight I sit in the saddle. I just have to work on pulling Sparkle up when I want her to slow down. Even though she's 16 years old, she's very forward moving. But that's why she's such a good sporting pony and I can't wait to see Josh ride her in the gymkhana on Sunday.

He was really sad to sell her, but she's too small for him now. His new horse Tara, is beautiful, but Josh says that Sparkle is the best sporting pony and he's really keen to do well in the gymkhana. Anyway, I agreed to let him take her this Sunday so he can compete on her one last time. I can't wait to go and watch! I've never been to a gymkhana before; it's going to be so much fun.

And Ali said that we could go riding together tomorrow. That will be cool. She'll be able to give me a lesson and help me improve my riding. Mom said I can only ride in the small paddock though, until Sparkle and I get used to each other.

Ali and I are becoming really close; I think she's my best friend now. And it's fun sitting in our special tree. That's what we've decided to do now when we finish riding each day - take some snacks, climb up and sit in our special tree in the big paddock and just watch the horses grazing. Mom says I now have my very own saddle club. That's my favorite TV show but I never thought I'd have a saddle club of my own. IT'S TOTALLY COOL!

Sunday 29 September

Oh my gosh, today was AMAZING!!! Sparkle won 4 blue ribbons, 2 red and one green and Josh gave them all to me. I'm so happy!

Sparkle is the best sporting pony, I can't wait to do gymkhanas on her myself. That bounce pony looks like so much fun and Sparkle is really good at it. And she's so good at barrels as well. But the jumping was the best – Sparkle is such a good all-rounder! Of course, Josh is a really good rider and really pushed her on, but I know I'll be able to do that too. Especially on Sparkle. What a talented pony!

And she looked so pretty today. I spent all yesterday afternoon getting her ready. It was so much fun in the paddock with Ali. We bathed her with this special horsey shampoo that made her coat look really shiny and Ali showed me how to braid her mane and tail as well. It looked very professional, especially with the colored ribbon that we braided through it. And the brow band that Josh's Mom made for her looked terrific. She said that I can keep it and she's even going to make me another one with ribbon the colors of my pony club, when I eventually join.

I can't wait till school goes back and I can tell all my friends about her – they'll be so jealous! I wonder if I'd be able to take her to school for show and tell? Miss Johnson might let me!

Tuesday 2 October

I can't believe it! Cammie and Grace now have a horse too. They're the girls who moved in across the road recently and with all 4 of us, we can have a proper saddle club. Four girls in the one street all with horses. They have to share Rocket – that's the name of their new horse (apparently he's really fast).

We're planning to meet up in the big paddock tomorrow. They don't have anywhere to keep Rocket but Ali's mum said it's fine for him to stay in their paddock for the time being. We'll all be able to go riding together. Their dad knows heaps about horses as well. He grew up on a horse property, so I guess he'll teach them how to ride.

I'm having another riding lesson with Jane tomorrow. This time I'm going to work on my rising trot. Ali's been teaching me how to do it properly already, so I bet Jane will be surprised at how good I am.

Sparkle loves the new hay that we've bought – it's top quality grass hay and as soon as she sees me with it, she comes cantering over. She's such a beautiful pony, the other girls all think so as well. I'm so lucky to have a palomino – she's definitely the prettiest horse!

Friday 5 October

IT'S NOT FAIR! Ali is MY friend and the tree in the big paddock is OUR special tree! Now Cammie has come along and taken Ali off me. They spent the whole afternoon together in the paddock with the horses and Ali showed Cammie our tree. That's where I found them when I finally got home today after going to the saddlery with Mom. She bought me a brand new pink feed bucket that is really cool. I was so happy because I found lots of things that I'd like for my birthday as well. It's only a month away and Mom said that she'd think about them. Hopefully she'll go back and buy them for me. Anyway, I raced over to the paddock to show Sparkle and give her a banana and there they were...both Ali and Cammie up in our tree together. And the worst part was that they weren't even interested in me. It's probably because they're the same age and I'm younger but it's not fair – Ali is MY special friend!

Mom said that we'll all have to just get along and that I can spend time with Grace, who is more my age. But I'm really upset about Ali. I can see that she and Cammie are going to become best friends now. I liked it when it was just the two of us. Why did the other girls have to come along and spoil it all?

Sunday 7 October

It was really scary today! My friend Ella came over with her brother Tim just as I was getting ready to go for a ride. Anyway, Mom said they could come to the paddock with us to have a little ride themselves. They were so excited as neither of them had ever been on a horse before.

Mom put the saddle on while I did up the bridle (Mom still can't figure out how to put it on properly). We led Ella around the paddock first. She was having such a great time. Then Tim decided that he wanted a turn. To make it a bit more exciting, Mom got Sparkle to trot while she was leading her. But then all of a sudden she turned Sparkle to the left. It was a really sharp turn. Sparkle was fine but it made the saddle slip completely down to her side. She just kept trotting along, not worried in the slightest, but Tim was almost on the ground.

Mom hadn't done the girth up tightly enough! She should know by now that it gets loose after a few minutes of riding. We all thought it looked so funny with Tim hanging on like that. Sparkle wasn't going very fast and he was hanging on really tightly so he was actually okay. But he didn't think so! It scared him half to death. He was even shaking. I'd forgotten it was his first ride on a horse – EVER – and he just isn't used to it. I hope this doesn't put him off riding.

But it was what happened next that scared EVERYBODY! Someone must have left the gate open because Rocket had wandered into Sparkle's paddock. When he saw us all gathered around Tim and Sparkle, he got all stirred up and galloped over. All of a sudden, he did a huge kick and came SO close to kicking Ella in the head. His hooves looked like they just missed her!

She screamed and this made him go even crazier. I think it was the scariest thing I've ever seen! Just before that, all of us were laughing at Tim. Watching him slide down Sparkle's side while she trotted along looked pretty funny. But then in the blink of an eye Ella was almost being kicked in the head by a huge horse. Mom was still freaking out about it after dinner tonight – she said she can't stop thinking about what could have happened. I don't think she'll ever forget to tighten the girth again, that's for sure!

Actually, I don't think any of us will ever forget what happened today!

And now I have to go back to school tomorrow. At least I can see all my friends and tell them about Sparkle. (I don't want to tell them about the near accident though – they mightn't want to come over if I do).

As soon as I get home, I'm going to race over to

the paddock and give Sparkle a banana. I hope
we have some. I'd better go and check – if there's
none maybe Mom can get some more on her
way home from work.

Horse drawing by Dad, he is the artist in the family!

Monday 8 October

School was so boring today. I just wanted to come home to Sparkle. All I could think about was my baby. I told all my friends about her and they're so jealous! They all wish that they had a horse. Everyone wants to come over and have a ride. Mom said, maybe not just yet. She's still getting over what happened yesterday. At least Ella is okay – and Tim as well. Ella and I were laughing about what happened to him. That was the funniest thing. But he doesn't think so.

Sparkle loved her banana this afternoon. I didn't ride, I just patted her and watched her grazing. She's the prettiest horse! I could see Ali and Cammie with their horses over at Ali's place. They waved to me but didn't come over.

I knew they'd become best friends. I don't know where Grace was.

At least I have my baby – Sparkle…AND my darling cat Soxy – I know that THEY love me!!!!

Wednesday 10 October

Dad put an ad in the paper to see if we can agist our big paddock. If we can get someone to keep their horse here, the money will help to pay for Sparkle's feed and my riding lessons. And just tonight a lady rang. She's coming over tomorrow to have a look. Dad said that she has a daughter who needs somewhere to keep her horse. She has a friend with another 2 horses as well and she doesn't have anywhere to keep them either. The lady told Dad that the girls are both good riders. They're about 4 years older than me but he said she sounded very nice and he thinks this could work out really well. Maybe the girls will be able to help me with my riding? Maybe we'll even become good friends! That would be cool, especially now that Ali is spending all her time with Cammie and Grace. It will be so good to have some other horsey friends of my own.

I hope they're friendly and that they do decide to keep their horses here. I can't wait to meet them tomorrow. I wonder what their horses are like? I hope they get along with Sparkle!

Thursday 11 October

Shelley and Kate are super nice and their horses are gorgeous. They love our place and think it'll be perfect. This is going to be so cool. If I introduce them to Cammie, Grace and Ali, they might even be happy to include me again and that means we can have a real saddle club – there'll be so many of us. I just wish we had proper stables like in the Saddle Club TV show. That would be really cool. But instead, we have to cross over our creek to get to the horse paddocks and it's so far to walk, especially carrying all the tack. I'm glad Mom carries the saddle for me!

Shelley and Kate are going to bring their horses to our place on Saturday and we've planned to go riding together. This is so exciting, I can't wait! And they've even said that they'll pay me to feed their horses each day. That's so good because now I'll be able to save up and buy those really pretty jodhpurs that I saw at Saddle World last weekend. Mom said I'm going to have to get up even earlier in the mornings now, so that I'm ready for school on time. But I don't mind.

Saturday 13 October

Our place is just like the Saddle Club now! Shelley and Kate brought their horses over today and we all went riding together. Then we spent the afternoon bathing and grooming them. It's so much fun having girls at my house and doing all this horsey stuff together. It's way better than having to do it on my own. Mom says the problem with Cammie and Grace is that they're keeping their horses at Ali's and that's why they've become best friends. But I have my own special horsey friends now. And they're keeping their horses at my house.

This afternoon we all just got to hang out and talk about horses. Shelley has a bay and Kate has a chestnut. The other horse is a paint and he belongs to Kate as well, but she doesn't ride him much. Sparkle seems to get along with them all so that's really good. And now she has lots of horses in the paddocks around hers so she definitely won't get lonely.

We met Kate's dad today when he brought the horses over and he told us that we could borrow his horse trailer anytime. This means I might be able to go to pony club when it starts up again next year. Shelley and Kate have told me all about it and it sounds amazing! I can't wait for that!

Shelley and her horse, Millie

Sunday 14 October

A sound like thunder woke me up at 5:30 this morning. At first I couldn't work out what it was because I was still half asleep. But then I realized it was horses' hooves galloping past my bedroom window. I heard Mom and Dad running down the stairs so I jumped out of bed and ran up the driveway after them.

Shelley and Kate's horses had escaped from the paddock and ran down the hill and across the creek. There's not much water in it at the moment and it's easy to cross. They must have been trying to get out the front gate but luckily they found the big feed bins that we keep in the shed. At least that stopped them from going out onto the road! We found them up there stuffing themselves with whatever they could find. Luckily it was only chaff but Mom and Dad were in a panic. The horses were really excited and stirring each other up, especially Nugget. He's the paint and he seemed to be the ringleader.

Mom, Dad and I were all running around in our PJs, with lead ropes and some hay, trying to catch them all. Mom and Dad were NOT impressed - especially at 5:30 in the morning! It was so hard to catch them and calm them down. Luckily there were 3 of us – It took quite a while to get them under control and back in their paddock. Dad then had to fix the gate.

What a way to start the day!

Dad rang Tom (Kate's dad) and he said that Nugget is an escape artist. When Shelley and Kate came over this afternoon, they said that he's escaped from a lot of paddocks. Dad was annoyed because Tom hadn't told us that before. He's going to try to find somewhere else to keep Nugget now. This will be good because we don't want that happening again!

At least we all got to go for a ride. When we went over to the paddock, Ali, Cammie and Grace were riding at Ali's. Our paddock is the best one for riding in though because it's so big. I introduced them to Shelley and Kate and asked them if they wanted to ride with us. Ali, Cammie and Grace were SO nice to me. I could see that they really wanted to be friends with the older girls as well. But Cammie's probably a bit jealous – I know that she wants to keep Ali to herself.

It was heaps of fun with us all riding together though and hopefully now we can all meet up after school one day this week and go riding again – that will be awesome if we do!

I hope the girls get on okay. It'd be great if we can all become good friends!

Kate's paint - Nugget

The Escape Artitst!!!

Monday 15 October

When I got home from school today, I found that
Nugget was missing from the paddock. I was so
worried because I thought he'd escaped again
but then Dad told me they've found somewhere
else to keep him. Dad was really relieved and
said it would be less to worry about. It's also one
less horse for me to have to feed each morning
and night. But that means less money as well
and that's not good because I really want to be
able to buy those jodhpurs as soon as I can.

I'm really excited though because Tom, Kate's
Dad, brought a heap of horse jumps over and
put them in the paddock. Kate's horse Lulu is a
really good jumper and Kate loves jumping so
she wants to practice. Tom said that he'd teach
me how to jump on Sparkle as well. This is very
exciting – I really want to learn how to jump – it
looks like so much fun. It'll probably be scary at
first but Tom said I can just go over little jumps
until I become confident. I know that Sparkle is a
good jumper as well, so I'm sure she'll love it
too. This is so cool!!!

Wednesday 17 October

I had a great time this afternoon. There were actually all 6 of us riding in the paddock together and everyone was so friendly to each other. I was really worried about that, especially with Cammie and I didn't know how it would work out. But even though we're all different ages, we get on really well. Shelley is the oldest – she's 13, Kate and Ali are both 12, Cammie is 11 and Grace and I are both 9. (Well, I'll turn 9 in just over three weeks' time – and I can't wait)!

And I got to try jumping!!! Kate and Shelley were telling me what to do. They were only small jumps but I loved it and so did Sparkle. Her ears went forward and she didn't even hesitate. I love her so much!

I saw a beautiful Wintec saddle at the saddlery on the weekend as well and I really hope that Mom and Dad buy it for my birthday present. It'll be so much easier to jump in than the Western saddle I'm using now. Ali's mom said I could borrow that until I get my own saddle. It's a great one to learn in because it helps hold me in place and I have less chance of falling off. But it's hard to rise up properly when I go for a jump.

The new Wintecs are so pretty and Shelley has one. She says it's fantastic. I'd really like to get some chaps of my own as well. Ali has loaned me her old pair but she has new ones and they look so cool. I should have enough money soon, but I want to get those jodhpurs as well – there are so many things I want to buy. Maybe I should just put them on my Christmas list?

I wonder if I'll get a new saddle for my birthday? I hope so! I can't wait!!!

Saturday 20 October

Mom was the only one at home today but it was lucky that she was there. Kate was trotting Lulu down the hill so she could hose her down after riding but her hoof got caught in some wire fencing. It's part of a gate that Dad made and someone left it lying across the track. Kate said that Lulu panicked and got all tangled up in it. Kate fell off her and it was so lucky that she wasn't hurt but Lulu's legs were all cut to pieces.

Shelley ran down to the house to get Mom and they managed to untangle Lulu. But her legs were really badly cut and Mom had to call the vet. Thank goodness Lulu's going to be okay! Kate's not going to be able to ride her until she heals though and that could take a couple of weeks! Kate was really upset and rang her Dad. She said he got really angry and wants to talk to us about paying the vet bill.

Now Mom and Dad are upset – they don't want to have to pay someone else's vet bill! I don't know what's going to happen. I hope that the girls can still stay here. It's been so much better since they arrived - the others are so much nicer to me now and we're all able to ride together. It has to work out.

Monday 22 October

We had visitors this afternoon and they left the front gate open! I'd brought Sparkle down to graze on the nice grass around the house and when I went to check on her, I couldn't find her anywhere. I just knew that she'd probably walked up the driveway and out the gate.

Mom and I raced down the street looking for her. We were so worried that she might have wandered down towards the main road. We couldn't see her anywhere so we headed up to the horsey property at the end of our street in case she'd gone there but no one had seen her.

We had to look down every driveway and Mom was getting really stressed. Then we walked up Cammie and Grace's driveway and that was like climbing a mountain, it's so steep. It was the only place we hadn't been to though. Then all of a sudden we spotted her in amongst some bushes. But as soon as she saw us, she decided to bolt. I didn't think we were going to be able to catch her at all but luckily I took a banana with me. She just couldn't resist! Then we managed to get the halter and lead rope on her and walk her home.

I'm so glad we found her – I don't know what I would have done if she'd gone missing! We're going to have to put a sign on the gate so people close it when they come in, in future.

Mom and Dad can't believe so many things have gone wrong since Sparkle arrived. At least it's all sorted out with Kate's dad now. He came over and worked out the vet bill with Dad. He's blaming us for the wire gate that was lying across the track. We don't know whose fault that was but Dad's just going to give him free agistment for a couple of weeks. Anyway, he's happy with that. And thank goodness Lulu is going to be okay. She just has to rest for another 10 days or so and then Kate should be able to ride her again. I'm so pleased about that and so is Kate. It would be terrible to have a horse and not be able to ride her!

My baby. I'm so glad she's safe!!!

Wednesday 7 November

I just haven't had a chance to write lately – I've been so busy looking after all the horses - especially now that the girls want me to rug them. This keeps their coats looking nice and stops them from getting bitten. I really need to get a summer rug for Sparkle as well. It's so much extra work putting the rugs on and off, but at least the summer ones can stay on all day. They actually protect the horses and help to keep them cool. I didn't know that! I'll definitely have to get one for my baby!

I'm SO excited because this Sunday is my birthday!!! – Finally! And all my friends are coming over for a pool party sleepover on Saturday. I can't wait to show them Sparkle. Mom said that we'll be able to give them pony rides on the grass by the pool. She said that she'll put Sparkle on a lead rope and lead them around. I can't wait!

I wonder if I'll get that new saddle? Mom and Dad said they won't tell me what they've got for me. They said it's a surprise and I have to wait. I hope it's the Wintec! I'm so excited – I'm definitely not going to be able to sleep tonight.

Sunday 11 November

It was the BEST BIRTHDAY EVER!!!!!

My party was amazing! Everyone arrived yesterday afternoon and the first thing they wanted to do was see Sparkle – they think she's so pretty and they all wanted to pat and brush her. I think she loved the attention. They all loved riding her as well. Mom and I led them around on the lead rope. Of course we made sure that the girth was extra tight and everyone was safe. Most of them live in suburban houses and don't get to be on a property so they always enjoy coming to my house. It's so much better now that I have a horse though!

And Nate even gave them rides on his motorbike. He can be the best brother when he wants to be! I think he was proud to show off his new bike and was more than happy to give all my friends a double around our house. That's another great thing about Sparkle, she's totally bomb proof and doesn't get scared of anything really. Her last owner Josh, rode motorbikes too, so I guess she's become used to them. This is great because it doesn't bother her at all when Nate and his friends ride their bikes in the paddock near hers.

My party ended up being heaps of fun – we spent hours in the pool, jumping off our diving deck. It's the best thing and we were all lining up in a row, holding hands and jumping in together. Mom took some great action photos as well with us in mid-air – they're so cool! The trampoline by the pool is heaps of fun as well and everyone just loved it. Dad set up lights around the pool area and also a mirror ball in the gazebo with lots of black plastic for the lights to shine on. We had flame torches lit in the garden as well and it was so beautiful once it got dark. Everyone was commenting on how pretty it looked.

After dinner, we had a disco in the gazebo and the mirror ball and all the lights looked awesome. Everyone thinks I'm so lucky that my dad is a musician because he set up his big speakers for us and even some microphones with stands for us to sing. We had the music really loud and everyone was dancing and singing and having so much fun. We played really cool games as well like Freeze, where you have to stand still when the music stops and also the limbo.

Mom and Dad had set up our big family tent down on the grass and we all slept in there. What a great night – a bit squashy but we all managed to fit. Ali, Cammie, Grace and I talked about horsey stuff all night. We hardly got any sleep. I'm so glad they came – we're getting on really well now and Grace and I are becoming great friends. It's probably because we're more the same age. Everyone else was telling us to be quiet because they wanted to go to sleep. I guess we all eventually drifted off, but I'm sure it was really late when we did.

Then today, we spent pretty much the whole day in the pool – and singing on the microphones as well. Tina, my best friend from school wouldn't stop. Dad said that you could hear her all the way down our driveway and we're sure our neighbors were glad when she finally went home. I think she wants to be a rock star when she gets older. Hopefully her voice improves!

And then late this afternoon after everyone left, Mom and Dad gave me my present. And it's the WINTEC!! They wanted to wait until everyone had gone so we could have some special family time together. Oh my gosh, I was so excited when I saw what it was. It looks so shiny and new – especially after riding the old western style saddle that Ali's Mom has been lending me. I was so used to that.

I'm really going to look after my new saddle. It comes in a special protective bag that I can keep it in when I'm not riding. Mom said that Sparkle and I won't know ourselves – I'm sure that she's going to find it much more comfortable as well.

I can't wait to go riding tomorrow and show the girls. As soon as I get home from school I'm going to race over to the paddock and go for a ride.

I'm so lucky – it was the best birthday ever!!!

Tina being a rock star!!! Ha Ha Ha!

Monday 12 November

Just when everything seemed to be going well…

I found a huge cut and a bruise in the shape of a hoof on Sparkle's side. Shelly's horse, Millie has become the boss of the paddock and I'm sure she must have kicked Sparkle. Millie's such a bossy horse and so greedy at feed times. Even though she has food in her own feed bin, she wants Sparkle's as well. She races across the paddock with her ears back and kicks out at Sparkle so she can get her food. Then she races back to her own feed bin to eat that too! She's so greedy! And it's so hard to make sure each horse gets their share when Millie's in the paddock. I think I'm going to have to take Sparkle out and feed her on her own in future.

And now I can't even use my new Wintec because the cut on her side is right in the saddle area. So it'll hurt her too much to have a saddle on. I wonder how long it'll take for the cut to heal? Not too long I hope! I can't believe I won't be able to ride her and just when I have a brand new saddle as well. But Mom said…you get what you focus on! She's always saying that and the strange thing is, she's usually right. So now I'm going to focus on Sparkle getting better quickly so I can use the Wintec and take her for a ride. I bet she'll love the new saddle just as much as me.

I'm going to ask Mom and Dad if I can take the Wintec to school for show and tell – that would be really cool. I'm sure Miss Johnson won't mind. I think I'll ask her tomorrow.

I'm going to braid Sparkle's mane like this...

Thursday 15 November

Mom and Dad took me to school today with my new saddle so I could show my class. They really liked it and I had to tell everyone the names of all the parts and how to adjust the stirrups and all. A lot of the kids have never even ridden a horse before so they knew nothing about it. Miss Johnson's such an animal lover, she was really interested as well. She brings her dog to school sometimes. She's a really cute Bassett Hound, called Shelby. Miss Johnson isn't married and doesn't have any kids so Shelby's like her baby. She's such a well-behaved dog and we're allowed to pat her and play with her. She sits right beside Miss Johnson's desk while we're in class – she's so cute! Miss Johnson said that she'll take photos of each of us with Santa hats on holding Shelby and we can use the photos to make Christmas cards.

And also, the BEST news is that Miss Johnson said I can bring Sparkle to school one day next week. Dad said that he would bring her in Tom's trailer and Miss Johnson said he can drive the trailer straight onto the oval. Then we can unload her right there and the whole class can go and look at her. How awesome is that!!! Everyone is so excited! She's such a quiet pony and she loves people, so she'll be fine, I know it. They'll have to keep their distance though. Miss Johnson said we all have to stay safe and no one will be able to get close to her or pat her or anything, but that's okay. It'll just be great to show her to everyone. This is the best thing ever. I bet nobody has ever taken a pony to school for show and tell – not at my school anyway!

I can't wait for next week!

Miss Johnson's dog – isn't she gorgeous!

Saturday 17 November

Sparkle's cut has nearly healed but Jim (Cammie and Grace's Dad), said I should wait a few more days before I ride her. It wouldn't be fair to put a saddle on top of that cut – it would hurt her too much and probably make it bleed again, so I just have to wait. It was still fun though because Grace and I were watching the other girls practice their jumping today and we were able to reset the jumps for them when they knocked them down. It was so great watching Kate jump Lulu. Her legs have completely healed and she was flying over the jumps. She can jump over 3 feet – that is so high! I can't wait until I can do that on Sparkle!

Grace and Cammie are still sharing their horse, Rocket and Grace said that because I couldn't ride Sparkle, then she wouldn't ride today either. So we just hung around together in the paddock and had fun. We're becoming such good friends now – we get along really well. She came over and swam in the pool with me this afternoon as well – that was great fun too. I love having a best friend as a neighbor. I'm so lucky.

There are no boys in our street for Nate to play with though, just heaps of girls – and we're all horse mad! He gets annoyed about that and says it isn't fair – but Dad takes him surfing all the time and he goes off motorbike riding with his friends, so he still gets to have fun. Mom says that we're both so lucky to have a property where we can ride horses AND motor bikes.

Nate has tried riding Sparkle and he even had a lesson with Jane, the instructor. But he doesn't like horse riding much. He says that he feels much safer on his motorbike. Mom said it's because he has control of his bike but doesn't feel the same when he's on a horse. I think that motorbikes are scary to ride – not horses! It's okay when he doubles me, but I still get scared. I did try having a go on my own a couple of times and Dad said I just have to practice so I'm more confident. I might try it again – Nate loves it when I ride his bike. But I definitely prefer horses!

We got a great surprise today as well because Tom put some barrels in the paddock so we can practice barrel racing. He brought logs as well and said we can put the logs on the barrels to make more jumps. So now we'll be able to set up a proper jumping course. Ali said we should paint colored stripes on them. I asked Dad and he found some leftover paint in our shed for us to use. He repainted our house last year, so we have heaps of leftover paint and brushes. It was really fun and the barrels and logs look so good – some have blue and white stripes and some have pink and white (the pink was leftover from painting my bedroom).

Ali is really arty. She's so clever and has such great ideas. It was so much fun painting all the equipment together. She also said we should use the spare logs for bounce pony. And we even made some bending poles. Dad found some special thin poles that are perfect and he mixed up cement to put into ice cream containers so we could stand the poles in them.

Now there's so much for us to do rather than just ride around the paddocks. I can't wait to join pony club next year so I can go to gymkhanas and do all of the events. Kate and Shelley have competed in heaps of them and won so many medals and ribbons. I know that Sparkle is a really good sporting pony and she already knows how to do all of these things. As soon as I can ride her again, I'm going to practice on her.

Me on Nate's bike. It's so much scarier than riding a horse!!!

Sunday 18 November

We all met in the paddock again today and set up the jumps. The paint was dry so we could move the barrels and logs around. It looks so cool and now we have our own jumping course. The girls came up with the BEST idea as well. We're going to have our own gymkhana right here in our paddock. We can organize all the events and do jumping, barrels, bounce pony and bending. Ali's going to make some ribbons for the winners and we're going to ask all the parents to come and watch. Kate and Shelley are going to work out a program and get it all typed up so it's really official.

This will be so cool and Mom and Dad think it's a great idea as well. I can't wait!

Shelley with Millie

Tuesday 20 November

Finally, Sparkle's cut has healed and I was able to ride her today. The Wintec is so awesome! It's so comfortable and Sparkle looks perfect with it on her back. It's so much nicer than the shabby old western saddle I was using. Mom says I have to be very grateful that Ali's mom loaned it to me though. And I really am! I think I'll make her a thank you card and take it over to her tomorrow. I think she'll like that.

The Wintec is so much easier to jump in as well. And today I even managed a 2 foot high jump. I'm so proud of myself and of Sparkle too. She's such a good pony and I love watching her ears go forward when she goes over the jumps. I think she loves jumping just as much as me! I have to practice keeping my eyes straight ahead though, facing in the direction that I want her to go. Ali was in the paddock this afternoon helping me – it's so good to have someone telling me what I'm doing wrong. Mom said that I'll learn so much quicker this way. Mom always picks up the jumps if Sparkle knocks any down. She's always in the paddock with me when I ride. She helps me to tack up and tightens the girth when it gets loose. (She'll never forget that again!)

I had the best ride today! After jumping I had a go at barrels, bending and even bounce pony.

Sparkle knows exactly what to do. I just have to push her on using my leg aids. She's pretty fast and I'm becoming so much more confident.

I'm going to keep practicing every afternoon if I can, so I'll be ready for our gymkhana. We'll probably have it in a couple of weeks. We have to work out a day when all the girls and the parents are free. Hopefully we'll be able to have it soon.

Oh and the best news as well – Miss Johnson told me today that I can bring Sparkle to school any day this week. I just have to check when Dad can get some time off work to take her. This is so exciting! I can't believe I'll get to take my pony to school for show and tell!

I love jumping!

Thursday 22 November

Oh my gosh!!! Today was incredible. Dad brought Sparkle to school in the horse trailer. It was during the morning session before the morning tea play break. He drove the trailer onto the oval and unloaded her right there. My whole class went down to look at her but Miss Johnson made everyone stand right back, just to be safe.

She asked me to demonstrate how to groom and brush her and how to clean her hooves with the hoof pick. Dad held her lead rope and she just stood there so quietly the whole time. Then Miss Johnson just couldn't resist – she had to go and pat her and she thought she was beautiful. She even gave her a hug.

Then all the kids wanted to pat her too and Miss Johnson said it was okay because she could see how quiet Sparkle is. They all had turns patting her and she just stood there so quietly the whole time. Everyone adored her – she's so well-behaved. Miss Johnson was raving about how beautiful she is and I felt so proud!

Everyone said that it was the best show and tell they've ever seen. And so did Miss Johnson. I'm so lucky to have her for a teacher. And I'm so lucky to have Sparkle for a pony.

Tuesday 11 December

I can't believe it's been almost 3 whole weeks since I've had a chance to write! I never seem to get much time for my diary lately - things have been so hectic lately, especially with all the horses.

Grace now has her own pony – a beautiful 14 hand chestnut called, Trixie. So now she won't have to share Rocket with Cammie. They'll each have their own pony and this is perfect for our gymkhana. We've decided to have it on the Saturday after Christmas because everyone's busy until then.

I can't believe that Christmas is only 14 days away and the school holidays are almost here! In 3 days I'll have 6 weeks off school and I'll be able to spend every day with Sparkle. The girls and I are so excited. We have so much planned! We're going to have sleep-overs at each other's houses and go riding EVERY day. We'll have to get up really early to ride though because it's SO hot now. Yesterday was almost 100 degrees and way too hot for riding! But the early mornings are perfect and so are the late afternoons when it cools down. I think that's my favorite time. It's so good in summer because it gets dark so much later and we now have more time in the afternoons to ride.

I'm so glad we have a pool! It's so hot, we'll be able to go swimming every day. And Grace and Cammie are getting a pool put in too. They're hoping it'll be ready for Christmas.

And the best news is, they're now going to keep their two horses in our front paddock rather than at Ali's. Our front paddock is right across the road from their driveway and it's much quicker and easier for them to feed and look after their horses. So Dad is going to buy a heap of special wire and posts to fence the paddock for them. The money that Jim pays Dad for keeping Rocket and Trixie will help to pay for Sparkle. We've started giving her special food and it's really expensive. But she seems to be getting skinny and we don't know why. We're hoping that the new food will fatten her up and make her really healthy. I'm so happy because the girls will be at my house all the time now, instead of always being at Ali's. This is going to be so cool!

I can't wait for Christmas. My list this year is full of horsey stuff. I might even get those jodhpurs that I've been wanting. They're so expensive, I still haven't saved up enough to buy them myself. Luckily Ali has given me her old ones to wear and Mom even found some blue ones at the 2nd hand shop that almost look brand new. And they fit me perfectly! I'd love to have the brand new pair that I saw at Saddle World though. I know they still have them because I saw them when I was in there with Grace the other day. Maybe Santa will give them to me?

I can't wait!

Grace's new pony, Trixie. So pretty!

Tuesday 25 Dec

We had an awesome Christmas Day!

Nate and I got up at 5am and ran in to wake up Mom and Dad. But we had to wait for Nana to get up and make a cup of tea before we could start opening our presents. She always takes so long! She arrived a few days ago and she's staying for 2 weeks. I was really excited because I thought that she could come to the gymkhana, but Mom said that she probably won't be able to make it across our creek. She's pretty wobbly when she walks and needs some help. Mom said that she'll have to get her a special walker soon so that she can get around easily.

I got the best presents and Santa gave me the jodhpurs I wanted. They're exactly the same as the ones in Saddle World and they look so cool. I tried them on and they fit perfectly. I'm so glad that he got the size right!

I got a new pair of chaps as well – they're the same as Ali's. I've been wanting some like hers for ages. As well as that I got some new riding boots. Now I don't have to wear Ali's hand me downs - but Mom said that I should still keep them as a spare pair. It's always good to have a pair to lend to friends when they come over for a ride, so they'll be perfect for that.

I got a brand new grooming kit as well. Sparkle

stepped on my old one and the case is all broken, so now I'll have lots of brushes. When my friends come over there'll be plenty of brushes to groom Sparkle with. I also got a new purple lead rope. I've just been using a faded old green one that Josh's mom gave me when we brought Sparkle home. This one will look so much better!

I LOVE SPARKLE!!

It's funny because I got pretty much all horsey stuff and Nate got things for motorbike riding.

He also got a drum kit. Mom says that he's spoilt but Dad says that it's fair because I have Sparkle. Dad wants us all to be musicians and play instruments like him. Nate is really good on the guitar and I guess now, he'll have to learn the drums as well. He's so excited about it. At least he can play them in Dad's music room up at our shed. Lucky it's sound proof!

I made Sparkle a special mash for her Christmas breakfast. I chopped up apples and carrots and added her favorite – some mashed banana. Then I mixed it with oats and chaff and added some of her favorite grass hay. She thought it was delicious! You should have seen her licking her lips. It was so cute! She kept dropping bits on the ground but that made Sheba happy. I think she enjoyed it as much as Sparkle! Sheba's our golden retriever and she ÁLWAYS comes over to the paddock with me when I go to ride or feed Sparkle. She loves it and always has her nose in a bush somewhere. All we can see is her backside and tail poking out and her tail is always wagging. She's so happy just sniffing around looking to see what she can find. She's great in the paddock too and loves wandering around when I'm riding. The horses are used to her and don't mind her at all.

It's so funny because my cat Soxy - who is the most adorable ginger cat you've ever seen - has started coming over to the paddock with us.

Mom says it looks hilarious. There's me, Sheba and Soxy all walking together. I would have thought a cat would be scared of horses but Soxy loves it over there. When we get to the creek though, I have to carry him. He just sits there looking at me and waiting to be picked up. The creek is really low at the moment because we haven't had rain for ages. So he can jump across without getting wet. When there's more water in it though, I have to carefully cross by jumping from one big rock to another. Dad's going to get a proper crossing made soon. That'll be so much better. He's just worried about it getting washed away if the creek floods. This happens when there's lots of rain, but hopefully he'll be able to work something out.

I had the best Christmas! Mom, Dad, Nate and Nana loved the presents I gave them as well. It was great this year because I saved enough money from feeding all the horses and I could buy really good presents for everyone.

Now we've got the gymkhana to look forward to! We're going to have it next Saturday afternoon and that's actually New Year's Eve. The girls are all really excited and so am I!

I LOVE CHRISTMAS!

Tuesday 1 January

New Year's Day!

Yesterday we finally got to have our gymkhana. We spent all morning getting ready and we were so excited! The girls and I set up a really cool jumping course, the bending poles and also bounce pony. The paddock looked so good with all the colored stripes that we painted on the equipment. And we were so glad that the weather was fine! We were really worried because there's a cyclone up north and the weatherman said that heavy rain and flooding is on the way. But there was no sign of it at our place, just more beaming sunshine.

The parents started arriving at 3:00 in the afternoon. They all brought fold up chairs and we set them up under the shade of some trees. So they had a really good spot to sit. Dad even drove Nana around to Ali's place and set up a comfy chair for her in the shade so she could watch the gymkhana from there. They all brought some drinks and snacks and said they were getting ready to celebrate New Year's Eve.

It all started off really well. We each did the jumping course a couple of times. In the end we decided not to score each other, but just have fun. Tom was helping us all with our jumping and pretty much giving us each a jumping lesson as we went along. This was really cool because he knows a lot about jumping and was really helpful. Then everyone ended up getting a ribbon. Ali ended up making one for everyone!

Just as we were about to start the other events, we suddenly heard a scream. Cammie decided to take Rocket for a ride in the big paddock and for some reason, he bolted. Then almost in a flash I saw Cammie on the ground. She had fallen off Rocket and then he raced off up the hill. Everyone went running towards her in a panic – it was really scary!

I felt my heart stop and I couldn't move. I could see her lying on the ground but she was completely still. Her Dad bent over her and we just stood waiting – I was really hoping that she was okay. Then he moved away from her and she slowly stood up. She was shaken up and she was crying. I was praying that she wasn't hurt. We've heard terrible stories of people coming off horses and being badly injured and I didn't want that happening to Cammie.

She took her helmet off and sat down with all the parents. Tom then went to catch Rocket and we all rushed over to her – we were so worried, but thank goodness, she was fine. She told us to go on with the gymkhana, so we did but it kind of wasn't the same after that.

Then Shelley and Kate's parents said that they had to go and get ready for New Year's Eve. Cammie, Grace and Ali asked me if they could stay the night at my house. Their parents said that they might come over as well and have a barbecue with us. Mom and Dad said that this was a great idea.

The girls and I decided to set the tent up so we could camp out for the night, just like at my birthday party. So Dad helped us get organized and set up while Mom got the food ready. Thank goodness, Cammie wasn't hurt badly. She said that her wrist hurt a bit from the fall and she had some bruises on her hip, but that was all. She was so lucky!

I ended up having so much fun with the girls last night and Nate joined in as well. We had a nighttime swim in the pool and later on we all got torches and played spotlight. It gets so dark on our property at nighttime though and hiding in the bushes can get pretty scary. There was a lot of screaming going on, that's for sure! Then Mom and Dad gave us some sparklers and party poppers and we let them off right on midnight. We all counted down and then called out HAPPY NEW YEAR!!!!!

Finally we went to sleep in the tent. Mom and Dad had to get up during the night though because it started to rain and they wanted to check that we weren't getting wet. Then at about 6:00 this morning, Jim arrived to pick the girls up. That was so early for them to leave and the bad part was, I was left to clean up all the mess!

Now it's pouring with rain. Mom and Dad said that it's meant to get worse and there might even be flooding. I hope my baby is okay. I brought her down near the house this afternoon so she could graze on the nice grass. But there's thunder and lightning right now so I hope she's not getting spooked! I wish I had stables to keep her in, so she can stay nice and dry. I'm glad she now has a summer rug! That will help to protect her from some of the rain at least.

Oh no – the lights are flickering. This storm definitely seems to be getting worse. I hope we don't have a blackout! I don't think I'm going to be able to sleep tonight – I'm too worried about Sparkle! Maybe I should go and look for her and check that she's safe. I can't stop thinking about her. Is she going to be alright????

The rain won't stop! The creek is flooding!

I'm worried about Sparkle!!!

Book 2

Pony Club Adventures

Dedication

This story is dedicated to Linda, Glen and Alyce.
Without their ongoing, friendship, support and
generosity, many of the adventures in this series
would never have happened.

Shelley…at pony club

Wednesday 2 January

Last night was the scariest night of my life!!! I overheard Mom and Dad talking. They were saying that if the rain keeps up, the creek is definitely going to flood. I knew that if it did, Sparkle wouldn't be able to cross over to the big paddock to be near the other horses. If she wasn't near them during the storm, she'd be really scared. And if she got spooked in the storm, then she could be seriously hurt.

Mom and Dad were in the kitchen cooking dinner and Nate was watching TV. So I decided to sneak out the front door. I went downstairs, got my gumboots and a raincoat and grabbed Sparkle's halter and lead rope. I just had to go and find her!

It was absolutely pouring with rain and by that time, it was really dark. I wasn't scared at all though because all I could think of was my baby.

Mom and Dad have commented before on how brave I am. Our car was stuck up near the front gate once, because a huge tree had fallen across the drive in some gale force winds. And the next night, I walked all the way up there on my own in the pitch black darkness so I could get something out of the car. I can't even remember what it was now. But it didn't bother me at all. My brother Nate would never do that! He's even too scared to go downstairs at night on his own. He's such a chicken!

Luckily I had a torch with me when I went to look for Sparkle tonight though. Otherwise, I don't think I would've been able to find her. She was standing under a tree and I heard her whinny when she saw me. I know she was glad that I was there.

I got the halter and lead rope on her and led her down to the creek to the spot where we usually cross. There was so much rain, I couldn't see that well, even with Dad's big torch. But then all of a sudden my gumboots filled up with water. The creek was definitely getting higher and I had to go really slowly across the rocks. Sparkle was walking along with me – lucky she's such a bomb proof horse otherwise I don't think I would've been able to get her to cross.

Just as we were about half way, I felt the lead rope pull really hard! I looked back to see what had happened and realized Sparkle had slipped into the deeper part of the creek! My heart was thumping so hard, I could feel it pounding against my chest. But all I could think about was saving her. I was standing on the trail of rocks where we always cross and I could feel the water really pulling me – it was so strong! I had to grip so hard to keep myself from being washed in.

I called out – Sparkle! Sparkle! – She was neighing and neighing but all I could do was pull on the lead rope. I was so scared! Then all of a sudden she managed to scramble back up onto the rocks. I have no idea how she did that – but I'm so glad she did! I was so desperate to get her across the creek that I just kept on going. I knew that she trusted me and would follow me anywhere!

We kept going and finally made it to the other side. Then we had to climb the hill. It was really muddy and slippery and we kept sliding down - it was so hard to make our way up. I fell over but she kept going and that helped to pull me to my feet. I'm glad I was able to get up otherwise she would've dragged me through the mud. We got to the top and I took off her halter and lead rope then let her go. Straight away, she raced into the paddock looking for the other horses. I knew once she found them, she'd be ok.

Then I had to get back down the hill. I had to hang onto tree branches so I didn't go sliding down into the creek. I knew that I was totally covered in mud, but I didn't care. The creek was rising and I just wanted to get back home. It was such a struggle to keep my boots on and push against the force of all the rushing water.

I felt so glad when I finally made it to the other side! I rushed back across the grass and one of my boots came off as I was running. So I had to go back and find it. When I made it back to the house, I left my muddy boots and raincoat downstairs. Then I sneaked back in the front door and into my room to get changed. Just then, I could hear Mom calling me for dinner.

When she saw me, she said she'd been wandering around the house looking for me. She asked why my hair was all wet. Then I started to cry. I just couldn't help it! When she asked me what was wrong, I had to tell her. And she just stood there staring at me. She thought I'd been in my room the whole time.

Mom and Dad both said they were in shock thinking about what could have happened. They said that Sparkle could have dragged me into the creek or fallen on top of me or anything. They said that I could have been washed away and drowned! They said that they wouldn't have known where to look for me because they had no idea I'd even left the house.

Now I'm worried that Sparkle might have hurt her back when she slipped over.

I can't stop writing tonight. So much has happened and I just have to write about it all. Mom says that writing things down really helps when you're upset.

It all feels like a really bad dream – I can't

believe it happened. Just last night, I was having so much fun with my friends and tonight Sparkle and I could have drowned. I think that Mom and Dad are still in shock as well! At least they didn't get angry at me. I think they understand how I was feeling. And I think they're just glad that I'm safe!

Thursday 3 January

Thank goodness Sparkle is okay! We drove around to Ali's house today to check on her. With the creek flooded, it's the only way we can get to her paddock. I heard her nicker as soon as she saw me. She trotted straight over to where I was standing and nuzzled up to me. I think she knows that I saved her last night and now we're even closer than ever. I love her and she loves me. She's my best friend in the whole world!

Our whole grass area was flooded! ☹

Sunday 6 January

It's been really hectic this week. It's still pouring with rain and the creek is still way too high to cross. There's been flooding everywhere and some poor people have even had their houses go under water.

Nate's happy though because the cyclone up north is making the surf really big. And Dad's been taking him and his friend surfing nearly every day this week. Those huge waves look so scary, but Nate loves it! I can't work out why he's so scared of horse riding. Surfing and motorbike riding seem so much scarier to me! Dad's tried to teach me how to surf a couple of times, but I couldn't stand up. We took Grace with us to the beach one time and she stood up straight away. Dad said she has really good balance. I got annoyed because I couldn't do it and she could. I don't like surfing anyway. I'd much rather ride horses!!!

Anyway, Mom or Dad has to drive me around to Ali's every morning and afternoon to check on the horses and feed them. I wish our paddocks weren't across the creek! The paddocks are so muddy and sloshy and our poor babies have to just stand in the rain. Lucky there's the big tree in the paddock for them to shelter under and at least they all have rugs on to help protect them.

Millie now has mud fever though! That's because she's standing in mud all day. Shelley had to call the vet and he said that so many horses have this problem at the moment. It's because of all the rain. Her legs have got this terrible infection all over them, especially around her feet. Now, I have to put some special betadine spray on them twice a day to help it all heal. She has medicine to take as well and I have to mix it in her feed. Shelley comes to look after her when she can, but she lives too far away to come every day.

I'm so lucky that Sparkle has such good feet. Everyone says that about her. She doesn't even need horse shoes! That saves us a lot of money because we only have to get her hooves trimmed occasionally, rather than paying for new shoes all the time.

When's this rain going to stop? The weather man said it's not supposed to clear up for another few days yet. Nate's keen for the creek to go down so he can have some fun playing in there. When there's plenty of fresh rain water, he paddles around on our big surf ski. And last summer he even caught a turtle. But I just want to go riding. I miss hanging out in the paddock with all the girls and spending time with my baby. It's the school holidays and we're all stuck indoors. At least the Saddle Club is on TV twice a day during the holidays. I get to watch it in the morning AND in the afternoon. It's the best show ever!

Me on our rope swing last summer ☺

Thursday 10 January

FINALLY the rain stopped enough today for us to tack up and have a little ride. The paddocks are so wet though and the only place we could ride was up and down Ali's driveway. I had to give all my tack and my boots a good clean last night. They were covered in mold from all the wet weather - it was disgusting!

When Tom came down to check on Cammie and Grace's horses this afternoon, he told us that he's found a great place for us to ride. It's in the state forest and he said there's lots of great trails. Also, it's only about one mile from here and we can easily ride there and then back home again afterwards.

So next week, Tom is going to take us and show us the way. We need an adult to go with us, just to be safe. He doesn't have a horse of his own to ride but Ali's mom said that he can ride her horse, Bugsy. Her horse is called that because he always gets attacked by bugs - especially mosquitoes. She has to keep him rugged all the time when he's not being ridden. She also has to put this special stuff on him to keep the bugs away. It's like an animal insect repellent. I think I should use some on Sparkle as well because I've noticed some bites on her lately too. Ali's mom doesn't ride much and she likes to see Bugsy being exercised. She said that a long ride like that will be good for him.

My first ever real trail ride on Sparkle and all of us are going together.

This will be really cool.

I can't wait!

Wednesday 16 January

Today was awesome! We all met in the paddock at 6am. We had to be tacked up and ready because Tom wanted to get going as early as possible before it got hot. We all followed him down the driveway, out the gate and down our street. I was so excited! Then when we got to the main road, we all had to dismount and lead our horses because it's too dangerous to ride them along there. This part was really scary! There's not really a proper footpath on the side of the road to walk on, so we had to be really careful. It was especially scary when semi-trailers went past. It seemed like they were only about 3 feet away from us and we could feel the wind as they drove along. They seemed to be going so fast. Even though I was scared, I still felt safe though, because Sparkle is so bomb proof - nothing seems to spook her. Also, because we were with Tom.

It was quite a long way to get to the entrance of the state forest but when we headed off the main road, we could ride again. Sparkle got so excited. All the other horses were walking but she just wanted to trot. So I had to go in the lead. And she's got such a quick trot! Everyone comments on her trot, but I'm used to it.

When we got into the forest, we had to ride single file. Ali was in the lead, I was in the middle and Tom was at the back. This was so he could keep an eye on everyone. And it was heaps of fun!!! There were heaps of little logs on the track and we got to jump over them. It was so fun going over all those jumps. When we were about half way, we stopped to give the horses a rest and have a snack. I gave Sparkle my banana. She loved it!

When we were riding, Tom kept saying - how's it going down there? I was on the smallest pony of all of us and he was on the biggest. He was so much bigger than me. That must have looked really funny.

Then at the end of the trail, we had to walk back along the side of the road. It wasn't as scary this time. I think the horses were glad when we finally got home though. They were all pretty tired by the end of it. That's the longest ride I've ever been on and my legs were pretty sore too - and my bottom! They're even still sore now.

We can't wait to do it again. Tom said that we might even be able to go once a week. I think he enjoyed it as much as us. He grew up on a horsey property and always had his own pony when he was a kid. He's so happy that Cammie and Grace are riding now.

I want to have my own horsey property when I grow up and I'm going to teach my children how to ride. I think I'll always have horses. I can't imagine not riding!

I'm going to have lovely fenced paddocks like this when I grow up!

Sunday 20 January

Charlie's been bitten by a snake!!!!!!!!!!!!!!!!

I can't believe it! POOR ALI! She loves that horse so much! This is terrible!

When I went to feed Sparkle this morning, I saw Ali and her mom with a beach umbrella set up in Charlie's paddock. I thought…what's going on? So I went over to check and he was lying down on the ground.

Ali said she found bite marks and blood on his leg and they called the vet. He said it was definitely a snake and had to give Charlie a needle with anti-venom. He told them to leave Charlie where he was and watch him carefully. The vet came back this afternoon but he said that there was no change. He doesn't know if Charlie's going to live!

I think Ali will probably sleep with him in the paddock tonight. I know that I would, if it happened to Sparkle. I hope he's okay. POOR ALI!!!! AND POOR CHARLIE!!!!! I feel sorry for them. It's terrible seeing him just lying there.

I don't want him to die!

Monday 21 January

Charlie's been lying down in the same spot ALL day. The vet came 3 times to check on him. He said that Charlie seems to be improving but he won't stand up. He said that if he lives through tonight that he'll probably be ok.

I don't normally say prayers but I'm going to pray for Charlie tonight.

Please let him be okay!!!!!!!

Tuesday 22 January

He's still lying down and he still hasn't moved from that same spot! Ali's been with him nearly the whole time. They were up all through the night checking on him.

I can't believe it's been another whole day.

PLEASE LET HIM LIVE!!!!

Wednesday 23 January

Charlie had to be put down today.

He finally tried to stand up this morning but then he just collapsed. The vet said that it's because he's been lying down for 3 whole days. His muscles must have become really weak and the vet said that they just pulled away from the bone. He said that he would never be able to walk.

It's so sad.

Ali is really upset. We were all crying. I'm crying right now. This is the saddest day ever!

I think they're going to bury him in the paddock. What's Ali going to do without him?

Monday 4 February

I haven't wanted to write in my diary lately - I've been too sad about Charlie. They did bury him in the paddock and Ali's mom said they're going to plant a special tree right over his grave. That way, they'll be able to remember him forever. Not that Ali will ever forget him.

I'm back at school now. I have Miss Johnson again but that's good because she's so nice and she's a really great teacher. The whole class has stayed together and we're all so happy about that because we're all friends.

Ali said her mom has started looking for another horse for her. I hope she gets one soon. It's not the same when she's not riding with us. But Ali said she doesn't want another horse.

Tom's going to take us for another trail ride on Saturday. He's going to ride Ali's mom's horse again. Ali said that she doesn't want to go.

Saturday 9 February

We went for a trail ride this morning. Mom said that it was good for me to do something fun. I've been really sad since Charlie died and the trail ride helped to take my mind off him. The best news is that Ali is getting a new horse! His name is Bailey and her mom said that he's a beautiful 15 hand chestnut. He belongs to a friend of hers who doesn't have time to look after him. So she asked if Ali would like to take him. Ali didn't want to at first, because she's still so upset about Charlie. But her mom thought it would be the best thing if she were busy with another horse. So Ali agreed. I'm so glad. I'm sure it will help to cheer her up again – I hope so anyway.

I do have some really exciting news though. Pony Club sign on is next weekend! And Mom and Dad said I can go. I'm really looking forward to that!

Sunday 17 February

We went to Pony Club sign on today. Tom was there and he introduced us to the lady who runs it. She's so nice! She has 2 daughters of her own who ride as well. No one had their horses there or anything, but Mom and Dad had to sign some forms and pay the fees. Then we bought my uniform. On pony club days, we have to wear a maroon polo shirt with our pony club emblem on it. And any jodhpurs we want. But when we're competing at gymkhanas or other competitions, we have to wear cream joddies and a special woolen vest. It's a really nice dark maroon, because that's our pony club color. I was lucky because they had some 2nd hand uniforms and I was able to get a shirt and a tie. I also had to get a special maroon saddle cloth – that's the uniform that the horses have to have so people can tell what pony club they're from.

Pony club is on every second Sunday and the first day for the year is next Sunday.

I CAN'T WAIT!!!

Sunday 24 February

Pony Club is AWESOME!!!

Tom came over early this morning with Shelley and Kate to load their horses onto his float. He showed Dad how to hook it up properly and Dad followed him in his car. When they got to pony club and unloaded the horses, Dad brought the float back to our house. It's lucky we only live about 15 minutes away so it didn't take too long. I was standing in the driveway with Sparkle on a lead rope and all my tack, ready to get going. I just couldn't wait to get there!

I walked Sparkle onto the float with Mom and Dad helping me – luckily she went on first go and didn't even hesitate. Tom said that some people have trouble getting their horses on floats, but we watched him load Millie and Lulu. And he gave us some tips as well, so we kind of knew what to do.

When we got there, we unloaded Sparkle and tied her up to the fence with some bailing twine. Shelley and Kate saved me a spot next to them which was so cool. They said that's their spot, where they always tie up – and now it's my spot too!

They were so excited that I was there and couldn't wait to show me around and introduce me to everyone. I felt so proud wearing my new pony club shirt and being friends with Shelley and Kate. They were so nice to me and were helping me with everything. All the other girls seemed really nice too and it was just so exciting to be there with my own pony! There's a few boys who go, but not many.

First of all, we had to all line up in the arena and the instructors came around to check that we were tacked up properly and that our girths were tight enough. Then we were put into groups depending on how good a rider we are. I was with some other girls my age. I was so glad I didn't have to go with the beginners.

We were there for the whole day and rotated around all the activities. We practiced so many different things and I can tell that my riding has improved already. I loved it when we did the jumping and the instructors were so helpful. I only did small jumps but it was really fun!

The best part was when we did sporting events in the afternoon. They were timing us and Sparkle came second in the barrel racing. I was really happy! We practiced bounce pony and bending as well and she almost won those too. The instructors said that she's a great sporting pony!

Then at the end of the day, Shelly and Kate loaded their horses onto the float and Tom took them home. We just had to wait for him to bring the float back for us. He lives really close by, so he doesn't mind. I'm so lucky that he's letting us use his float or I wouldn't be able to do pony club at all. Ali, Cammie and Grace all want to go as well. But they don't have a float so they can't. I'm so lucky!

When we tried to load Sparkle this time though, she just wouldn't go on. Maybe she was tired and suddenly decided to be naughty? We kept trying and trying but she just refused. I didn't know horses could be so stubborn!

Luckily one of the instructors came and helped us. He showed us how to use a rope with 2 people holding each end and sort of wrapping it around the back of her while I led her on with the lead rope. Anyway, it worked and she went straight on. Everyone at pony club is really nice and helpful.

Just as we were leaving though, we got the fright of our lives – or Mom and Dad did anyway! When we were about to drive out onto the main road, we went over a speed bump and all of a sudden, there was a loud thumping noise. It was so lucky that Dad decided to get out and check because the horse float had come unhooked from the tow bar on our car. All that was keeping it attached was the metal chain.

Dad was able to get it hooked up properly so that it was all secure but it was so lucky that it came unstuck right there! If we'd driven out onto the main road, we would have had to go up a really big hill. And Dad said that the float would definitely have come off the car. If this happened, the float would have rolled down the hill into the cars behind us. Imagine that!!! My poor baby could have been killed and even the people in the cars as well.

That would have been a disaster! We were so lucky! Mom is still talking about what could have happened and how lucky we were! Dad's going to have to be so careful in future. He has to make sure the float is hooked up properly.

Mom and Dad don't want me to tell the girls. If Tom finds out, he mightn't lend us the float anymore.

But I don't want to think about that!

Pony club is THE BEST and I had THE BEST DAY EVER!!!!

I can't wait till we go again in 2 weeks' time.

I'm going to ride Sparkle every afternoon now and practice and practice. This will help to build up her muscle tone as well. She's going to look so good! I love going to Pony Club! It's cool!!!

Saturday 2 March

I've been riding every afternoon this week. I've been going later when it's really shady and not so hot. Mom's been helping me with all the sporting events. She's been using my watch to time me and I'm getting quicker every day, especially with bending and bounce pony. I've been going over bigger jumps too and now I can jump 27 inches!!! That's getting so much higher. Sparkle does seem to be getting stubborn though. Sometimes she just stops at the jumps and yesterday I nearly fell off. Ali told me that she's getting used to me and wants to be the boss. So now I have to really use my leg aids and push her on. I have to be really strong and push her over the jumps. I have to show her I'm the boss!

Tomorrow the girls and I are going to go for a big ride up on our neighbor's property. They have this massive hill and heaps of land and they told Dad that it's okay for us to ride up there. We just have to watch out for their cows. And of course, be sure to shut the gate so they don't get out. It's so pretty up there.

Sunday 3 March

Today we went through the gate onto our neighbor's big hill and the view from the top was AMAZING!!! We could see for miles and miles and there are beautiful green hills everywhere – it's so nice for riding! And we could see the Andalusian horse property just down the hill. So we decided to canter down and have a look. It was so much fun and the Andalusians are so pretty.

But then, we came across all the cows. And they had little calves with them. They were so cute. We wanted to get closer and have a look but Millie was petrified. She's such a big horse - but she's such a huge scaredy cat! She's scared of EVERYTHING!!! Even crossing our creek when there's hardly any water in it. She will not cross over it! She has to jump across. And that's a huge leap! It's scary watching her.

Anyway, when Millie got scared of all the cows today, Shelly had trouble keeping her calm. And then all of a sudden, some bulls appeared out of nowhere. This one bull just came for us! I was so scared because it started chasing us and we had to gallop down the hill to get away. And the hill was so steep – it was scary getting down. I was petrified!

Shelley told me later that it was the scariest

moment of her life. She thought when the bull was chasing us, we'd get pinned to the fence. It was SO SCARY!!!

We couldn't get back into our paddock quickly enough! My heart is still thumping just thinking about it.

Such a shame about the bulls. The little calves were so cute!

Monday 4 March

When we got home from school this afternoon, there was a cow in our driveway. We couldn't work out where it had come from. But then when we got down to our house, we found there were cows everywhere.

They were all over the grass – there must have been at least 20 of them!

Dad thought we must have left the gate open yesterday afternoon and that's how they got in. But I knew that we'd definitely shut it properly. We didn't want to risk that bull coming in our paddock after us, that's for sure!

But when I went over the creek to the horse paddock to check, there were no cows in there at all – thank goodness – or Millie would have gone crazy.

Dad said they must have got in through the fence somewhere down near the house. But the problem was he couldn't get hold of Matt, our neighbor, to help him chase them out again. We all tried, but they just ran around on our grass and then pretty much ignored us. I think they love our grass. It really is the best grass – that's why I bring Sparkle down to graze. I hope they don't eat it all!

I shone a torch down over the balcony tonight

and I could see a pair of huge eyes shining up at me. There was a cow laying down right by the house. Dad's just worried they'll destroy our garden. At least we couldn't see any bulls.

Our dog Sheba keeps barking at them. And I think that Soxy is too scared to go out at all. At least that'll stop him from trying to hunt wildlife! He's the cutest most adorable cat you've ever seen, but he's been so naughty at night time lately. Mom said that we're going to have to lock him in after dark from now on.

I can hear those cows mooing. I hope they don't keep us awake!

This is the cow we chased off our driveway.

Tuesday 5 March

Well, we woke up this morning, hoping the cows would be gone but they were still there. They started mooing at sunrise. We weren't happy!

At least Dad managed to get hold of Matt this afternoon and he came over and helped Dad chase them out, back over to his property. He said he found where they managed to get in and was going to mend that part of the fence.

I hope they don't get in again. Our lawn is wrecked now! It was still soft from all the rain we've had lately and now there's big potholes everywhere from their hooves. There's huge cow paddies everywhere too. I hope Dad doesn't expect me to clean all that up! I have enough horse manure to pick up as it is!

Sunday 10 March

Pony Club again today! It was fun! Dad dropped us there and then took Nate surfing. Sheba went with them. She loves going to the beach. She spends all day trying to catch fish. Mom stayed with me at pony club – because a parent always has to stay – and plus Mom loves watching me ride. Then Dad, Nate and Sheba came back for us this afternoon.

The girls are all nice and I've made a new friend called Kelly. She's a bit older than me but she's so friendly. I love it when we stop for a lunch break and everyone just hangs out together near the clubhouse. And they make the best food. Today, they cooked burgers for everyone and they were so delicious. Everyone is always so hungry and all the food gets eaten, which is good. This helps to raise money for the pony club so they can buy new equipment and pay for some really good instructors to come and teach us.

We had a big meeting as well and they told us that our pony club gymkhana will be on Sunday 12 May. That's less than 2 months away. And that'll be my very first gymkhana! I'm so excited! I can't wait!!!!

I'm going to practice on Sparkle as much as I can – this will be cool!!!

Saturday 16 March

So much happened today!

First of all, Dad rang Jim to find out when he's going to put Cammie and Grace's horses in our front paddock. It's been so long now since Dad bought everything for the fencing and Jim even spent a day helping to put it all up. But then today, he told Dad that he's going to keep their horses at Ali's. Dad wasn't happy because it cost him a lot of money and he only put the fence up to help Jim out. And I wasn't happy, because I was looking forward to the girls keeping their horses at my place.

Then Tom arrived with their float to pick up Kate's horse Lulu. He said that he's found a great horse property to keep her on and has decided to move her. This was more terrible news, because I didn't want Kate or Lulu to go anywhere else. And I was worried that Shelley might move as well. Then I'd be left with no one.

On top of that, I was really worried because I didn't know what would happen with Tom's float. Would I still be able to use it? Without his float, I can't get to pony club and Mom and Dad have already bought all my uniforms.

But luckily, Tom is kind and generous. He said that we can still borrow it. All we have to do is drive to his house to pick it up on pony club days. I was very glad! It would have been terrible otherwise. So now, Shelley and I will take our horses together – this will be heaps of fun!

Then just when I thought everything was going to be okay….Ali's mom and my Dad nearly started a huge bushfire!!!

Ali's mom has told us that we should burn off our small paddock – she's done this before and it can help get rid of any bad grass and weeds that are growing. Our property used to be used for cattle and our paddocks are full of a type of grass called setaria. This is good for cows but not horses. If they eat the white husks off the top, they can end up with a disease called "big head." This makes their heads get all swollen and makes them really sick. So we have to slash the grass with a big tractor type mower to keep the setaria really short and get rid of the white husks. Anyway, she suggested that burning off would really help and said that she would show us the best way to do it.

So she poured petrol in rows down the paddock and Dad set it alight. Before we knew it, there were rows of fire across our small paddock. But then all of a sudden the wind came up. It started blowing flames everywhere and I got really scared. Mom and Dad said that they were really worried as well. We were just about to call the

94

fire brigade, but somehow, Dad managed to get it all under control.

What a day! Now we have a burnt paddock and one less horse because Lulu is gone. And as well as that, we have brand new fencing around our front paddock but no horses to keep in it.

But at least, we can still use Tom's float and we can still get to pony club. It would be terrible if we couldn't do that!

I don't want Lulu to go!! ☹

Wednesday 20 March

Dad was at the hardware and stock feeds store in town today and saw an ad on the noticeboard. Someone is looking for a place to agist their 2 horses and he took their phone number so he could call them.

Anyway, it turns out that it's a lady who has a horse and also a little Welsh Mountain pony. The pony belongs to her daughter who's the same age as me. Well, she's just turned 10 and I'll be 10 at the end of the year, so it's close enough!

Dad said that they're coming over tomorrow afternoon to meet us and have a look. If it works out, he's planning for them to keep their horses in our front paddock. That way, the paddock will get used after all.

I'm excited because it's someone else who's around my age. And I haven't been seeing any of the girls much lately. So it would be so nice to have someone else to ride with.

I wonder what she's like and what their horses are like? Dad didn't really ask, so now I have to wait until I get home from school tomorrow. I searched for some photos of Welsh Mountain ponies because I didn't know what they look like. They're very cute. I wonder what hers is like? I can't wait to meet them!

Thursday 21 March

The girl's name is Nikita and her mum's name is Jo. Jo has a 15 hand grey called Billie and Nikita has a Welsh Mountain pony called Cappy. He's only 10 hands high so he must be really small. The only worry is that because he's so little, he might actually escape by going under the fence.

Anyway, they're keen to keep them here and they're going to bring them over on Sunday. Nikita seemed very shy, but nice and Dad talked to Jo about us two girls riding together.

At least I won't have the smallest pony anymore! Yayyyy!

Saturday 23 March

Cappy is the cutest pony I've ever seen! All the girls came over to have a look at him this afternoon after Jo and Nikita left. They all think he's cute as well. I'm really glad that they're keeping their horses here. The front paddock seems perfect for them. We think that Cappy should be okay but we'll have to keep the front gate shut just in case he does manage to escape.

I just love his shaggy mane and forelock – it's very long, it even partly covers his eyes. But he is the cutest thing ever. Nikita said that his coat gets really thick and shaggy in winter as well. We all think he's just adorable!

Dad talked to Jo again about us girls going riding together. I was too shy to ask Nikita and she's shy as well, but hopefully we can. She's really pretty and she seems really nice. Maybe I'll see her tomorrow afternoon when we get back from pony club.

I have to clean all my tack now because the instructors give us points for having clean tack. Dad said at least that will make me look after everything. I'm going to put on a Saddle Club DVD and clean it all while I'm watching the show. I'm up to a really good episode – I can't wait to see what happens.

Sunday 24 March

I couldn't go to pony club today!!! It was the worst thing ever!! Sparkle would NOT go on the float! Shelley couldn't go because she was sick, so it was just me taking Sparkle. Dad drove all the way to Tom's house to get the float, but we couldn't get her to walk on. We tried everything! Even using the rope trick didn't help. She was really stubborn, she just refused!

I was really disappointed. I've been so looking forward to it. And I even cleaned all my tack and everything last night! After about an hour of trying, I just had to take her back to the paddock. There was nothing else we could do because we had no one to help us. By that time though, I didn't want to ride and there was no one to ride with anyway. I was so keen to practice all the events for the gymkhana today too. I really need to work on my rider class and they were going to have a special instructor there today as well.

I'm just going to have to practice in the paddock every afternoon. Even if it's on my own. I really need to get Sparkle ready for the gymkhana. It's only about 6 weeks away and it'll be here before I know it. But now we have to work out how to get her on the float. When Dad took it back to Tom this morning, he said it usually helps if another horse gets on, then the 2nd one will follow. So maybe if Shelley and I go together, she can put Millie on first. But then, I heard Shelley complaining the other day that she's even having trouble getting Millie on the float. So I don't know what we're going to do.

At least I saw Nikita this afternoon when she came with her mom to feed their horses. We arranged to have a ride together next weekend, so that will be fun. I'll be able to take her over to the big paddock so we can ride there. She hasn't seen Sparkle yet. I can't wait to show her off.

He's the cutest little pony ever!!

Saturday 30 March

Nikita and her mum, Jo came over today. They were hoping to go riding in the big paddock but it's been raining all week and it's way too wet over there. None of us have been able to ride at all this week.

Anyway, Jim suggested we all go down to the vacant block of land at the end of our street. There's probably a couple of acres there and he walked down this morning to have a look. Luckily for us, it's nowhere near as wet as our paddocks. So we all decided to tack up and go down there for a ride.

I could see that Nikita was really shy because she didn't really know anyone. So I walked along on Sparkle right next to her and Cappy. Mom was chatting with Jo. Then Nikita and I started chatting as well. She goes to a different pony club to me and she was telling me all about it. I told her that my pony club's gymkhana is coming up soon and she said that she'll probably go to that. She said she loves going to gymkhanas.

She said that her pony club is going to have a gymkhana soon as well. She thinks it's maybe a month after mine. Each of the different pony clubs holds their own gymkhana and this means I can go to lots of them this year. This will be so fun. As long as I can get Sparkle on the float!!

Nikita and I had a great time riding around the vacant block together. We just trotted and cantered around and followed each other. Cappy is so little. Everyone loves him. He gets along well with Sparkle too. It's amazing because Nikita told me that he's actually a really good jumper. I'm sure he's really good at sporting because he's so small and quick, but it's hard to imagine such a little pony going over big jumps. I can't wait to see her jump him.

When we got back home and untacked the horses, Nikita came down to the house with me to look at our baby chickens. She is such an animal lover and I knew that she'd really like to see them. It was so cute, because they'd escaped from the pen Dad made and were down on the grass with Sheba. They've got used to her because she sits by their pen every day. I think she feels like she's their mom. It's really cute!

Nikita is really nice. I think we're going to become good friends!

Saturday 6 April

Nikita's mom, Jo rang us last Sunday night. She said she's heard about a horse trainer who might be able to come out and help us with loading Sparkle on the float. Apparently he's helped lots of horses with the same problem.

We told Shelley about him as well and her parents were keen to ask him to help Millie too. So Dad called him straight away and arranged for him to come this weekend. We were so glad that he was available. Today, Dad had to go to Tom's to borrow his float so the trainer could use it when he arrived this afternoon.

We couldn't believe how quickly he trained Sparkle! It only took him about 4 goes and she was walking on and off the float without a problem. It was amazing! He got me to practice with her and she was so good. I was able to get her on and off easily!

After he worked with Millie on the float, Shelley asked him to help with getting her across the creek as well. She's too scared to walk over the rocks and always jumps across. But this is so dangerous. Millie is such a scaredy cat and it took him a long time! Eventually, he was able to get her to cross. He said that it doesn't usually take this long when he's working with horses but that every horse is different. Millie is just a big chicken!

The best news is that now, Shelley and I will be able to go to pony club tomorrow because we'll be able to get Sparkle and Millie on the float - easily. The forecast is for fine weather and we can't wait. We're both really excited. It's been a whole month since we last went and we can't wait to go again. Hopefully the rider class instructor will be there. I need to practice for the gymkhana!

Shelley and Millie at pony club

Sunday 7 April

Sparkle walked straight onto the float today – both this morning on the way to pony club and this afternoon when we were leaving. It was easy peasy! I'm so proud of her. Millie still seems a bit scared but when she sees Sparkle go on, then she walks on too.

And it was a really fun day! The rider class instructor was awesome and she was really impressed with my riding. I felt so proud of myself. I also got to go in the same jumping group as Kelly this afternoon. That was really fun because she's a really great girl! Shelley and Kate are usually in different groups to me so I only get to catch up with them during lunch breaks.

The instructor was helping me get Sparkle over the jumps. She's still being a bit stubborn and refuses the jumps sometimes. But I'm improving at being really firm with her and that helps a lot.

At the end of the day, we all hosed our horses down, tied them up and gave them some feed. I gave Sparkle a biscuit of hay as well as some special feed in her bucket. I'm still trying to fatten her up but it's taking a while. Then we got to just hang out in the clubhouse while all the parents sat around and chatted.

I just LOVE pony club. It's the best!

Monday 6 May

I can't believe a whole month has passed since I've had a chance to write in my diary! I've been so busy working with Sparkle to get her ready for the gymkhana and now it's only 6 days away. Mom has been coming over to the paddock with me every afternoon and timing me on the barrels, bounce pony and bending. Sparkle is getting so much quicker at everything.

I can't wait until next weekend! Shelley and I have decided to spend all day on Saturday getting our horses ready. We're going to bathe them and groom them so their coats are really shiny. Then Shelley's going to show me how to braid Sparkle's mane and tail. Mom's going to buy some maroon and cream ribbon because these are our pony club colors. And I'm going to thread the ribbon through her tail and also her mane. I've got the really pretty maroon and cream brow band that Josh's mom made for me as well. Sparkle is going to look great.

And the great news is, Shelley's parents decided to buy their own float. They ordered it a while ago and it's finally ready for them to pick up. They're going to keep it here at our place and they said that I can use it for Sparkle any time I want. That is nice of them and I'm really lucky!!! Now Dad doesn't have to drive to Tom's house all the time to borrow his. I don't think he was very happy about us using it all the time anyway. So, I'm very lucky that Shelley is getting one of her own. And she's going to keep it here. That will make everything so much easier!

Cammie, Grace and Ali still don't have a float to use – so they can't go anywhere – except walk to the state forest for a trail ride.

I'm lucky - and I can't wait for the weekend!!!!!!

Saturday 11 May

I loved today. We bathed and groomed the horses and their coats look so shiny now. The braiding took quite a while – Shelley showed Mom and I a special way to braid the mane and it's quite tricky, especially threading the colored ribbon through. I'm glad Mom was helping me. We also painted their hooves with special hoof paint. I used a shiny clear one on Sparkle and her hooves look so much better. Shelley said that some girls even put special make up on their horses. I can't believe that! Make up on a horse!! That's mainly for shows though – when they want to cover up any marks and make their horses look absolutely perfect.

When we finished the grooming – which took us all afternoon - we put their rugs on to keep them nice and clean. This will help to keep the braiding in place as well. And tonight we're keeping them under the house. There's such a big area there that's fenced off, so we can keep them in. I guess it's kind of like a stable and because they're together, they won't get scared. This way, we can keep them from rolling around on the grass or in any mud. So they should still be lovely and clean in the morning.

I need to go and clean all my tack now and get it as shiny as possible.

I can't wait till tomorrow. I'll have to be up really early so that I'm ready in time. I can't wait to wear my special shirt and vest. I'll have to get Dad to do my tie up for me.

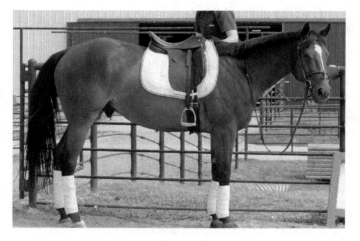

I wonder if this show pony wears make-up?

Sunday 12 May

Today was the best day of my life!!! Shelley got here really early this morning and we got all our tack together as well as biscuits of hay and buckets of feed for our babies. Then we loaded Millie and Sparkle onto the float. Thank goodness Sparkle is fine now and goes on and off without any trouble at all. Millie still gets scared but as long as Sparkle goes on first, then she just follows.

When we got to pony club, there were horse trailers everywhere. Luckily no one had taken our special spot, so we were able to park there and tack up next to Kate. I was so excited and we could tell that the horses were getting excited as well. They both looked so beautiful with their manes and tails braided and their shiny coats. I felt so proud in my special competition uniform as well.

First of all we had the march past and all the horses from each club walked around the arena in groups. Our horses looked so smart. The colors of our pony club really stood out and definitely looked the best! Mom said that we deserved to win. It was such a great way to start the day!

Then all the riders had to go into their age groups for the events. Nikita was there competing and so was her mom, Jo. Jo went with the seniors, Nikita went in the Under11's group and I went in the Under 10's group. That's because my birthday is so late in the year and I won't turn 10 until then.

There were 12 riders in my group all from different clubs. I was feeling so nervous and I think Sparkle was nervous too. Mom and Dad were nearby watching and Dad had our video camera. He always has the video camera – he videos everything!

My first event was bending and I was really excited because I know how good Sparkle is at this. When the gun fired, she took off so quickly and we raced around each pole. I knew that I'd gone really fast but we had to wait until everyone had their turn before the winners were announced. They gave out the ribbons straight away…white for 5th place, yellow for 4th, green for 3rd, red for 2nd and blue for 1st. And I was given the green! I was very happy! My very first gymkhana event and I had won a ribbon!!! I felt great!

My next event was bounce pony and Sparkle raced over all the logs without knocking any off. In this event I came 2nd. So I had a green and a red ribbon.

After that it was the keyhole race. I've never

done that before, so I waited to go last. This way I could watch the other riders to see how it's done. The first 3 were disqualified because they rode out of the key. I could see that I needed to do sharp turns but Sparkle is really good at those, so I was hoping she'd do well.

When it was finally my turn, we raced down the straight part, around the key hole and then back again. There was so much cheering and I could hear people calling out my name. Ali, Cammie and Grace had turned up to watch and got there just in time to see me go. Nate was there as well as Mom and Dad and they were all cheering me on.

The judge gave me the blue ribbon! I couldn't believe it. Everyone was crowding around me saying congratulations! Another girl even commented to her mom about how lucky I was to have so many people watching me and cheering for me. She told her mum that I had my very own cheer squad. And I guess she was right. I felt really proud!

The next event was jumping. I got really nervous about this one and I guess that Sparkle could sense it. I pushed her on and made sure I looked straight ahead to where I wanted her to go. There were some really good jumpers in my group so it was pretty tough. Sparkle knocked over a jump which made me lose points and she refused a jump as well. I had to turn around and take her towards it again. She went over it the second time, but that slowed me down a fair bit. I didn't get a ribbon for that event, but Dad asked the judge and she said that I had come 6th. Everyone said that this was really impressive for my very first jumping competition. I was so pleased with myself and with Sparkle.

The girl who won the red ribbon for jumping, shocked everyone! When the judge handed it to her, she threw it down on the ground and said - it's not good enough! She then got down off her horse and screamed out – STUPID HORSE! Then she walked off in a big huff. We were all so shocked! We've never seen anything like that before. Her mom had to grab her horse's reins so he didn't run away. I think her mom was really embarrassed. I don't think I'll ever forget that girl. What a way to behave!

There were so many different events and I won ribbons in nearly all of them. Mom was carrying them for me and there were so many. I think my favorite event of the day though was Mystery. A lot of the horses get scared in this because they have to race over all these mysterious surfaces, like plastic tarpaulins and old tyres and also go through steamers and curtains that have been strung up around the trees. But Sparkle is so bomb proof that nothing seems to spook her. I was able to get her through the whole event without any problem. Poor Shelly couldn't even finish it on Millie when her group went through because Millie was so scared. I think she stopped at the plastic tarp and would not go any further. Poor Shelley! Anyway, Sparkle came 2nd so I got another red ribbon. I was really happy!

At the end of the gymkhana was the presentation. This is where they add up all the points that each person gets in their age group. It turned out that I came 4th in my age group overall and I won a trophy!!! I was so excited, I couldn't believe it! My very first gymkhana ever and I won a trophy.

I was happy driving home. We were all talking about it and Mom and Dad were really proud of me. My ribbons and trophies are so pretty – I'm going to put them somewhere special in my room so I can look at them every day. I think I'll take them to school for show and tell tomorrow. I can't wait to show everyone.

I'm proud of my baby! She's the best pony EVER!!!

Saturday 18 May

Everyone at school loved my ribbons and trophy. Miss Johnson was really interested in the events at the gymkhana and she asked me to explain them all to the class. They thought it was really cool and asked me if I get scared when I jump.

Mom has asked me that as well. I'm not scared but it makes me nervous when Sparkle refuses to go over. I was practicing my jumping today and it wasn't much fun. She kept stopping at the jumps and I had so much trouble trying to get her over any of them. I have to grip so hard because I'm really worried that I'm going to fall off. I've only fallen off her once so far and that's because I was being silly when the girls and I were riding in the paddock one time last year. I was kind of bouncing around in the saddle and laughing and mucking around. And I wasn't holding the reins properly. She kind of made a really quick movement – maybe something spooked her or maybe it was because of me being silly. Anyway, all of a sudden I was on the ground. It really gave me a fright. I didn't hurt myself too much but it was hard not to cry. And I didn't want to get back on.

Ali's mom told me I should though. She said that the best thing is to get straight back up in the saddle. I really didn't want to but all the girls were watching me. I was feeling really embarrassed about it all. They kept asking me if I was alright. But this just made me more embarrassed. In the end, I decided I'd better hop back on – it would be too embarrassing not to!

Mom said that she was really worried when she saw me fall. But at least I wasn't hurt and it certainly taught me a lesson. I'll never be silly on a horse again, that's for sure.

Anyway, it's pony club tomorrow and I'll be able to practice my jumping there. I hope that Sparkle behaves. I'm going to give her some extra special feed tonight to make sure she has plenty of energy.

I can't wait to see everyone.

Sunday 19 May

I couldn't wait to get there today. Shelley and I were the first to arrive, so we had plenty of time to get the horses tacked up and ready. It was such a beautiful day and I couldn't wait to get started. We've been bringing Sheba to pony club each time we go now. Other people bring their dogs too, but I know that all the girls like Sheba the best! She loves all the attention she gets when she goes there. And the new trick that Dad taught her is so funny. He points his finger as if it's a gun and says – Bang, Bang - then she rolls over onto her back and pretends that she's dead. Everyone loves that trick and they're always trying to get her to do it.

When I hopped on Sparkle, she seemed just as excited as me. I could tell she was looking forward to the day too. We went off into our groups and I did rider class first. I'm working on getting her to use the correct lead when she canters. This is really important and if she's not doing it properly, I'll never do well in that event at gymkhanas. I'm still learning how to get her to do it. And I'm not sure if she is or not, so I have to ask Mom to tell me. The instructor said that when you get really good at it, you can feel the difference when you're riding and you'll know if it's right or not. I'll just have to keep practicing.

We did lots of different training exercises in the different arenas and that was really fun. Then we all stopped for a lunch break. It was such a hot day today, so everyone was glad to have a rest and something to drink and eat. I bet the horses were too.

After lunch, most of the girls chose to do jumping. I was nervous about this because Sparkle's been so naughty at it lately. I managed to get her over the first jump so that made me feel better. It was only a little one though, but it was a good start. They gradually made the jumps higher and Sparkle started off behaving well. I was pushing her on and I could see her ears going forward. I think she was enjoying it too.

Then they raised the jumps some more. But Sparkle was being so good that I felt really confident. I turned her towards the first one and just as we got close she suddenly stopped. I felt myself flying forwards and I had to grip so hard to stop myself from coming off. It was really scary. The instructor told me to try again. I felt really nervous especially with everyone watching. I took her towards the jump and she did exactly the same thing. It was so hard to stay in the saddle and I could feel my thigh muscles aching from gripping so tightly. Then I tried one more time. I think I was expecting it and sure enough, she stopped again. But this time was so sudden, that I could not stay on. I felt myself flying through the air and then I hit the ground. I knocked the jump off with my arm as I fell and came down right on top of it. Everyone came running over to see if I was ok. I felt a bit dazed and my arm really hurt. The worst part though was that it was so embarrassing! I hated everyone staring at me. And it was hard not to cry!

I didn't want to do any more. So I took her out of the ring, untacked her and hosed her down.

She's being naughty and I don't know what to do!

Now I have a really sore arm from where I fell. Dad said that it's a wonder I didn't get seriously injured. He was amazed that I was able to get up and just walk away.

The instructor told him that we should get Sparkle looked at. He said that maybe she has an injury and is in pain or maybe the saddle is hurting her. But it can't be the saddle – it's my new Wintec and I only just got it for my birthday last year! Someone else said that maybe she's just being naughty and needs a trainer to get her to behave.

Dad said that he's going to call Alice who owns the Andalusian horse property down the end of our street. She's a horse trainer and also a Bowen therapist for horses. Dad said that he'll call to see if she can come and have a look at Sparkle. Apparently Bowen therapy is a special type of massage that even humans can have done when they have sore muscles or problems with their body. Hopefully she'll be able to work out what's wrong.

I wonder if she is sore or if it's the saddle causing all the problems. Or if she's just being naughty!

I hope that Alice can come soon so that Sparkle gets back to normal. I just want her to be the way she used to be!

This is exactly what happened to me today!!

Monday 20 May

This afternoon, I found Sparkle lying down in the paddock. At first I thought she was just resting, but when she saw me she would not get up. And when she sees me with her feed bin, she always comes trotting over. I started to panic. It reminded me of seeing Charlie lying down in his paddock after the snake bite. I thought - Oh no! Not a snake! Not my baby!

I went running over to her, but she wouldn't move. She was breathing. But she just laid there looking at me. My poor Sparkle – I didn't know what to do! I started crying and I could hear myself saying – Sparkle! Sparkle! Please don't die!!!

I didn't want to leave her but there was no one in the paddock to help me. So I had to run down to the house to get Mom and Dad. My heart was thumping so badly, I almost couldn't breathe!

They raced back over to the paddock with me. I couldn't get there quickly enough. As soon as Mom saw Sparkle, she tried calling the vet. But he wasn't available! The other 2 vets we know of were on other calls as well and couldn't come till much later. We couldn't believe it! Mom had to keep trying until she finally found someone else. He told her he would come straight away and that he would be here as quickly as possible. He said we should just stay with Sparkle and keep her calm.

I was in such a panic. I was trying to be strong and not cry. She couldn't die! I wasn't going to let her. I thought if I talk to her it would help. So I ran my fingers through her mane and stroked her neck. I told her how special she is to me and that I can't live without her. I told her that she has to stay strong and get better. I told her that she's the best pony in the world and that I love her.

She just looked at me with her beautiful, big, brown eyes and I knew that she was listening.

Finally the vet came. He said she has an infection because her temperature is really high. But he's not sure what's causing it. He gave her an injection with some really strong antibiotics. He said we should cover her with a rug and just keep her calm. He said that there's nothing else he can do at the moment and that he'll come back in a few hours to check on her again.

I've been sitting with her in the paddock. Mom and Dad kept coming over to check on me - and on Sparkle. Dad finally said I have to come down to the house – he's with her now and he thinks I'm eating dinner.

But I'm not hungry! I don't want dinner – I just want to stay with my baby!

I'm going to go back over now to be with her. The vet should be back soon and I want to be there when he comes.

Sparkle, I love you.

Please get better!!!

Tuesday 21 May

The nickering I could hear as I tumbled out of bed this morning, had to be Sparkle's. It's amazing how well noise carries across the paddocks and I knew that I would recognize that sound anywhere. She has a different tone to the other horses and I always know when it's her. Mom says it's just like being a parent. They always seem to recognize the sound of their own child's voice above all the others. And it's the same with me and my baby.

The vet finally came back last night after what seemed like hours of waiting. Even though Mom and Dad kept insisting that I go back to the house, there was no way I was going to leave her on her own. The only way they could coax me to get some rest was if Dad promised to stay with her. But I knew I wouldn't get any sleep. How was that going to be possible when my baby was so sick? I didn't even know if she would survive the night!

As I raced over to the paddock this morning, my heart was thumping wildly and the same words kept going around in my head – Please let her be okay! Please let her be okay!

I could not get across the creek and up the hill quickly enough. But when I finally reached the point where I could see her, I just couldn't stop my tears from falling.

I've been having constant visions of Ali's horse Charlie, lying deathly still on the ground after being bitten by a snake earlier this year. He was in such a bad way, that after 3 days of being unable to stand, his muscles completely gave way and he had to be put down. This was my biggest fear with Sparkle when I couldn't get her onto her feet yesterday.

But after a night of rest and several doses of really strong antibiotics, she was actually not only standing but walking towards me! My baby was alive and I knew in my heart that she was going to be ok.

I gently stroked her neck and she nuzzled up to me. I felt so grateful right then. I thought I was the luckiest girl ever! But when the vet came to check on her later this morning, he said that she's been suffering from a serious flu virus. And that she's really lucky to have survived. He said that she's going to need lots of rest and some special attention for a while. I am more than happy to do that for her but I was not prepared for what he told me next.

Her sporting days are over. He said that along with the flu virus, which will take quite a while for her to recover properly from, she's also developed chronic arthritis. And the kindest thing to do would be to retire her in the paddock, with some occasional gentle riding. I couldn't believe what I was hearing! What about pony club? What about competing in gymkhanas? What about improving my jumping? He said all of that will definitely be out of the question for her now. And that she will more than likely refuse if I even try to get her over a jump.

So that explains why she's been so stubborn and naughty lately! It's just been too painful for her to even attempt jumping. I've had no idea! Thank goodness there's some medicine I can give her to help with that now, so that she won't feel so sore. As long as I hardly ride her that is.

I'm so glad she's ok, but what am I going to do? How will I be able to cope without riding? Horses and riding are my entire world now. I have to be able to ride!

After hearing that news, I refused to go to school today! I just wanted to stay with my baby. And I was way too upset to be going anywhere. Mom thought I needed to stay at home and rest, but when I ran into my room, I couldn't stop crying!

It's not fair!

Wednesday 22 May

I hardly slept at all last night and I did not want to go to school again today. But Mom said I had to. When I checked on Sparkle before leaving to catch the bus though, she seemed to be quite content. I wonder if the arthritis medicine is working already. Hopefully it is! The vet said that it's an anti-inflammatory which will help to stop the pain. She was happily grazing when I got home this afternoon as well. It's almost like she was never sick.

When I finished checking her over, I spotted Ali, Cammie and Grace all tacking up to go for a ride. They were planning to practice their jumping but I didn't stay and watch. The thought of it just brought tears to my eyes.

And I know they're planning another trail ride in the state forest on the weekend. But what am I supposed to do? Shelley's keen to go as well, so I guess I'll just be stuck here on my own – unless Nikita comes over to ride Cappy. I hope she does. At least I'll have Sparkle to keep me company. Mom keeps telling me to be grateful that she's still alive. And I am!!! But it's just not the same.

Thursday 23 May

I can't believe what Mom and Dad are planning! They haven't told me this before, but ever since Sparkle started refusing jumps and being naughty, they've been looking in the paper for another horse that's easier to handle. And now that I really can't ride her much anymore, they said that as soon as her health starts to improve, we need to sell her or give her away. And in the meantime, start looking for another horse.

I can't believe they would even think about doing this! How can I sell my baby? I can't just get rid of her! How can they even think that I would want to do that?

Having 2 horses to look after would cost too much money. That's what Mom and Dad say, anyway. It's not fair! I would love to have a new horse to ride but I have to be able to keep Sparkle!!

What am I going to do?

Saturday 25 May

The girls all went for a trail ride early this morning. I could hear their voices and laughter when they got back. I'm sure they had the best time. I didn't want to go over there though, it's too upsetting. It's not fair that I can't ride.

I went to check on Sparkle later this morning when no one else was around. She seems to be recovering really well. She was so happy to see me and nuzzled my hands and pockets looking for treats. It's the cutest thing when she does that.

I sat under the big tree and just watched her grazing. Sheba came over to keep me company and laid down in the shade next to me. I'm so lucky to have such a beautiful dog. Everyone adores her! But she sure is getting fat now. It's only a few weeks until her puppies arrive. Mom and Dad suggested a few months ago that we should let her have a litter. And they decided to look for another pure bred golden retriever to breed her with. When we saw how protective of our baby chickens she was, we knew she'd be a great mom. We're sure she thought the chicks were actually her babies. I'm really looking forward to the puppies arriving. A litter of little retriever puppies will be so cute!

I've been thinking a lot today and I've come up with a plan! I'm going to start looking for a new pony. Then I'm going to convince Mom and Dad to let me keep Sparkle as well. I'll do lots of chores so I get more pocket money and I can help pay for her feed. It's the arthritis supplements and special feed for her that cost the most. But I have lots of birthday money saved up, so maybe I can use some of that. And hopefully because Sparkle's getting older, no one will want to take her anyway. I'm sure it'll all work out. Mom always says – you get what you focus on – so that's what I'm going to focus on now...getting a beautiful new pony AND keeping Sparkle.

I think I'll get on the computer right now and check to see what ponies are for sale.

Sunday 26 May

Last night, I found 3 horses that look like they'll be just perfect. It's really hard because there's so many beautiful ponies for sale but they're either too far away for us to go and look at – some are even in other states – or they're just not the right type of horse for me.

I made a checklist of all the different things I need in a horse.

First of all, I don't want one that's too big or too small. Probably between 14 and 15 hands would be good.

The age is important – somewhere between 8 and 14, I guess. Definitely no older!

I also want a horse that's good at sporting because I LOVE gymkhanas and I really want to go in lots of them this year.

And I want a good jumper, because I'd like to do lots of jumping.

I guess an all-rounder type of horse would be perfect. That way, I'll be able to do lots of different styles of riding. I'd love to try eventing – that would be so cool!

As well as that, I want one that has a nice quiet nature and isn't hard to pull up.

I know that's a lot to ask for, but there are 3 horses on horseyard.com that pretty much fit the description I'm looking for AND they're not too far away. I'm so glad Nikita told me about that site – that's where her mom found her latest horse and she's so happy with him.

Sparkle has become hard work lately and even though I haven't wanted to admit this before, it hasn't been a lot of fun riding her. Cammie and Grace's dad, Jim says I should get a gelding. He says that they are definitely much calmer to work with and have less attitude than mares.

Anyway, the 3 horses that I've picked out actually are geldings and they look so pretty as well. Mom said that she'll call the owners tonight and have a chat with them. Hopefully, we'll be able to go and have a look on the weekend.

This is really exciting! I can't wait!!

Wednesday 29 May

Mom's managed to speak to the owners of all 3 horses that I picked out. One of the ponies sold on the weekend, which is a shame because he sounded really nice. But we're going to look at the other 2 on Saturday.

I really hope that one of them is the horse for me. Pony club is on Sunday but I can't go because I don't have a horse to ride. So the sooner I find one, the better!

Saturday 1 June

I was so excited for today, but then in the car, I started getting really nervous. It's kind of scary hopping on horses that you don't know and then having people stand around watching you ride. It's really nerve-wracking! You kind of feel like they're judging your riding while they're watching you.

Anyway, maybe Beau picked up on the way I was feeling. That's the first horse I tried. The owners told us that he's like a big teddy bear, but he certainly wasn't like that for me, that's for sure. He started pig rooting and being really naughty. I got scared and had to hop off. Mom and Dad told the owner, that he's probably not right for me. I wouldn't want him anyway! It's amazing what people say when they're trying to sell their horses. Beau was definitely no teddy bear! He was even naughty for the owner when she hopped on him. And then she tried to make excuses for why he was behaving like that.

We've heard horror stories about what some owners do. Sometimes they even drug their horses so they're well-behaved when people try them out. But then when they get them home, they go psycho!! It's pretty scary when you think about it. You have to be so careful when you're buying a horse.

The next horse was named Duke. And that name suited him so much. Mom said that he was kind of regal looking and knew that he was beautiful. The girl who owns Duke used to show him and did quite well but now she has a new horse that's a really good jumper. That's what she wants to get into.

Duke was lovely to ride and seemed like he had a really nice nature. And he was gorgeous looking as well. But he's not a sporting pony – he's definitely meant for the show ring. Mom and Dad were annoyed because we drove so far and wasted a whole day looking at horses that were nothing like what I wanted. It's such a shame that the other one sold. I bet he would have been perfect.

Now I have to keep looking for something else. I hope I can find a pony soon. I'll have to try some other websites and Dad said that he'll check the paper.

Fingers crossed – we'll find the perfect pony this week. I hope so anyway!

Book 3

Dream Pony

Wednesday 5 June

The most amazing thing happened tonight! Dad opened the local paper and found a 14.2 hand, 11-year-old, chestnut all-rounder advertised for sale. He said he wasn't actually planning to look for horses, but for some reason, the ad just seemed to jump out at him.

Anyway, when he rang the owner, he could not believe who he was speaking to! It turned out to be Josh's mom, Tracey. They're the people who we bought Sparkle off! What a coincidence!! Mom said that it's just meant to be! Tracey is the nicest lady ever and she was really helpful when we were buying Sparkle. She said that she's really sad to be selling Tara – that's the horse's name - but Josh just doesn't ride anymore. She said that Tara's going to waste in their paddock and that she's way too good a horse for that.

And the best part is, she sounds PERFECT!!!!

I know she's a mare, but Tracey says that she's absolutely beautiful and has the nicest nature ever.

We're going to look at her tomorrow afternoon.

I'm SO excited!!

TARA! TARA! TARA! TARA! TARA! TARA! TARA! TARA!

What a lovely name!

She's going to be the one!

I JUST KNOW IT!!!

This is the photo they emailed me. She looks SOOO pretty!!

Thursday 6 June

Tara is the loveliest horse! As soon as I hopped on her, I knew straight away that she was going to be perfect. She's really calm, has a lovely soft mouth and is really easy to pull up. I tried her over some jumps and she didn't even hesitate. I think she's going to be a perfect all-rounder. And Tracey says that she's totally suitable for beginners right through to advanced riders. She's an ideal size for me as well and even as I get taller, she won't be too small. I love her gentle nature - I can see why Tracey is sad to be selling her.

And she's really good at sporting. Tracey showed us the trophies and ribbons that Josh and Tara have won in gymkhanas. There's heaps of them!! That is so cool!

As well as all of that, Tracey said that Tara is a very good doer! She's really rounded and easily keeps weight on just by grazing in the paddock. They hardly have to give her any extra feed at all. This is great! Especially with all the money it costs us to feed Sparkle.

After Mom and Dad chatted with Tracey for a while, they suddenly decided to pay a holding deposit. It all happened so quickly. Mom was reluctant to decide straight away, but they could see how much I love her and how perfect she is.

And they were also worried she might sell. There's a lady wanting to look at her on the weekend - it would be terrible if she was sold to someone else. Anyway, we're going back tomorrow for another look, just to be sure.

Tracey said that she would love to have had a daughter who is horse mad like me. Josh is a good rider but she said he always preferred motorbikes.

Tara is SO pretty! I really don't know how he can sell her, but I'm glad he is. Tracey said that the money will go straight into his bank account. I wonder if he'll spend it on a new bike?

Oh my gosh! I know this is going to work out perfectly. I'm getting a beautiful new pony called Tara. This is a dream come true.

I'm going to call the girls right now and tell them all. I can't wait for them to see her! Tracey said that she can bring her to our house on Saturday.

I CAN'T WAIT!!!!!

Saturday 8 June

I can't believe that I actually have a new pony!

I was really excited when Tracey unloaded her this afternoon. She is just beautiful! And she goes on and off the float easily. She crossed the creek without any trouble as well. I put her in the small paddock next to Sparkle and Millie, just so they can adjust to each other over the fence. They were so cute – they walked over to say hello to her straight away – I'm sure they'll all get along really well.

I think Tracey was really sad to say goodbye. Mom said that she thought Tracey was going to cry. She's keen to watch us compete in some gymkhanas, so at least she'll still get to see Tara. And she's going to make me some more brow bands as well. That's so nice of her! She's such a nice lady! I told her that I'll call and let her know how Tara is going. She's really glad that we've bought her – she said she knows that Tara will be in good hands.

I spent the rest of the afternoon in the paddock, just watching her graze. I'm going to have to be careful not to neglect Sparkle now – or she might get jealous. Ali, Cammie and Grace all came over to see my new pony and they think she's beautiful as well. I can't wait to show Shelley and Nikita. And I can't wait to go riding on her!

I thought I should just let her settle in today and give her time to get used to her new home.

I still adore Sparkle and she'll always be my baby, but she has such a quick little trot and is quite hard to pull up. Tara seems a lot easier to ride.

I'm the luckiest girl ever!!

Tara…in our paddock ☺

Sunday 9 June

I had so much fun today. Tara is absolutely awesome!!! I just love her!

She's so easy to pull up and really willing to do whatever I ask her. I tried her with bending and bounce pony and she's really good at both of them. And it was lovely to jump her as well. She didn't shy away from the jumps even once. Her ears go straight forward and I'm sure she loves jumping as much as me.

Her trot is perfect too and really easy to rise to. I just love riding her.

Nikita came over today with her mom Jo and they were very impressed. Jo asked me all about her and wanted to know where I'd found her – as soon as she saw her, she commented on how lovely she is.

I felt so proud.

She really is a dream pony.

I can't wait to take her to pony club next weekend. They're all going to love her too, I know it!!

Monday 10 June

Shelley came over this afternoon and we rode in the big paddock together. Tara was really well-behaved and Shelley's very impressed with her. I knew she would be.

After my ride, I put Tara and Sparkle in the paddock together and they just couldn't wait to be near each other. They seem to get on really well. I think they've already become attached. It's crazy though – Tara's much bigger and rounder than Sparkle but I hardly have to feed her at all. Tracey told me how much to give her and I couldn't believe it! Sparkle has to have nearly a full bucket of feed every night plus a biscuit of hay twice a day as well. But Tara only needs a small amount each night, or she might get too fat. The complete opposite of Sparkle! I'm giving Tara hay as well though! I can't give some to Sparkle and not Tara – that wouldn't be fair.

I'll always love Sparkle – she's my first pony and she's very special. But Tara is definitely my dream pony. And I know I'll get to keep them both!

I'm so happy!!!!

Wednesday 12 June

The most incredible thing happened yesterday afternoon. Mom got home from work and went looking for Sheba. We've been keeping a close check on her lately because we knew the puppies would be due soon - Mom actually thought that there was one more week to go. Anyway, she finally found Sheba in her kennel and when she called her, she wouldn't come out. So Mom said that she bent down to look inside and make sure she was okay. And when she did, she got the surprise of her life. Sheba was having her puppies!! Right then, right while Mom was watching. How incredible is that! I wish we were at home then, but we hadn't got home from school yet. I'm glad in a way that we were late though, because one of them died. Mom said that it was stillborn. That is so sad. That poor little puppy. When Dad came home, she got him to take it away before we saw it.

But the good news is, Sheba has 9 of the cutest little puppies you've ever seen in your entire life!!!! I don't think there could be anything cuter than golden retriever puppies. And 9 of them! Oh my gosh, Sheba is going to be really busy and so are we! We had to move them into a special enclosure that Dad had ready. That was where they were supposed to be born, but I guess Sheba felt more comfortable having them in her kennel.

One of them is sick though. Dad said that there's often a runt in every litter. But we're going to try to save him. He's so little and sweet and we have to make sure that he gets his turn at feeding. All the other pups just barge their way in so they don't miss out. But he's too weak to look after himself. I hope that we can save him and I'm really glad that Mom and Dad want to try. They're even setting the alarm tonight, so they can get up and make sure he gets fed.

Luckily we've been collecting newspapers for a while because we're sure going to need a lot. 9 puppies make a lot of mess! I've had to change the newspaper 4 times already today and I'll have to do it again before I go to bed. At least I was allowed to have the day off school. Mom and Dad said because this is such a special occasion, we should all have the day off.

This is so cool and I can't wait to show the girls. Nikita is especially going to love them. I think she's the biggest animal lover of all of us – except for maybe Shelley. She absolutely adores our pets – she's not allowed to have a cat or a dog because her dad's allergic to their hair. So she loves coming to our place to play with Sheba and Socks. Wait till she sees the puppies!

I'd better go and check on them.

I hope we don't run out of newspaper!

Thursday 13 June

I did not want to go to school today! I just
wanted to stay with Sheba and her pups. They
are really, really cute. I can't believe how cute
they are! And Sheba is such a protective mom.
She watches every move we make. So we can't
take them too far away from her just yet. They
still have their eyes closed and they're just
adorable. It's keeping me really busy though,
because each pup has to be weighed every day.
This is to make sure they're putting on weight
and getting enough milk. It's impossible to tell
them apart though, so we've had to put different
colored wool around their necks. I made up a
chart today to keep a record of who is gaining
weight and how much they've grown. The
hardest part was thinking of names for them all!
It was very hard to come up with 9 different
names.

Tina is what we've called the little one and she's
hardly growing at all. Where as all the others
have grown heaps already. I hope that she
survives – it would be really sad if she doesn't.

The girls came over to have a look and they
think that they're just gorgeous. Nikita stayed all
afternoon after her ride. We're becoming such
good friends and tomorrow we're going to have
a ride together. I'm really looking forward to
that!

Friday 14 June

Nikita and I rode together in the big paddock this afternoon and practiced our jumping. Cappy's so little and cute. It's incredible that he can jump the height that he does! I think Nikita cleared almost 36 inches on him today.

I can't wait to take Tara to pony club on Sunday. I wish Nikita and I went to the same one. That would be awesome if we did.

I got some bad news tonight though! Well, it's terrible for me! When Jo came to pick Nikita up, she told us they're moving their horses on the weekend. I couldn't believe it when I heard! There's not enough grass in our front paddock so Jo has found somewhere else to keep them. Just when Nikita and I have started becoming close and having heaps of fun together. And Cappy is the cutest little pony – I don't want him to go either!

I'm really sad about this. I was hoping that we could go riding together all the time. Nikita is my age and we get on really well. It'd be okay if we went to the same pony club, but we don't.

Dad told Jo that us girls will have to get together sometime and Jo agreed. Hopefully we'll be able to ride again soon. I'm really going to miss Nikita and Cappy! We'll all miss Cappy. I don't think I've ever seen a pony as cute as him!

Saturday 15 June

It was the funniest thing ever today! Mom, Dad and I all told Nate that he should have a ride on Tara. He wasn't that keen because he's tried riding Sparkle – he even had a couple of lessons – but he didn't really enjoy it very much. I think it's because she's so forward moving and hard to pull up at times, so he was probably a bit scared. But Tara is very different. As Tracey said, she's perfect for any level of rider, including beginners. So after a bit of coaxing, he finally agreed.

The problem is that we don't have a riding helmet to fit him. He has such a big head and there's no way he can get my helmet on. When he rode Sparkle, he borrowed one off the instructor. After that, Mom said there's no point buying one for him if he's not going to ride. So anyway, because he didn't have one to wear today, he wore his motor bike helmet. And it looked so funny!!! We were all cracking up laughing. But Nate didn't care – he was actually having the time of his life. He got so confident, that he tried to get her to canter. That didn't last long though. I don't think he was too sure of that. And it was really funny watching him trying to do a rising trot.

After a while, he decided to even try some small jumps. Tara was just brilliant. She is so willing to do whatever her rider asks of her, that this wasn't a problem at all. And because Nate is such a dare devil and used to going over massive jumps on his motor bike, he thought jumping a horse was great fun!

But I know it's because he was riding my dream pony. I'm becoming so attached to her. She's not only beautiful on the outside, but she's so gorgeous on the inside as well. No wonder Tracey didn't want to sell her!

I think I should call Tracey tonight and let her know how well it's all going. She'll be pleased to hear how happy Tara is, I'm sure.

I also need to get my tack cleaned ready for pony club tomorrow. I definitely want Tara to look her best when we walk into the arena.

I can't wait to get there!!!

Sunday 16 June

Today was absolutely awesome! As soon as I arrived, Kate's dad, Tom came straight over to look at Tara. And he was SO impressed. He told me I have a really good horse now and that she would be an excellent endurance pony. That's what he loves doing and said that he'd love to take her on an endurance ride himself. I didn't know much about this before, but apparently they go on rides for miles and miles and ride all day long – with a few rests along the way of course. Sometimes they even camp overnight with the horses and then continue riding for the whole next day. He said that Tara would be a great endurance horse.

So I guess this means that she won't find pony club tiring and I'll be able to do lots of riding on her without wearing her out. This is another great thing about her!

I felt very proud when I walked her into the arena. Her coat looked really glossy and shiny in the sun and my tack was perfectly clean. The instructors always check to make sure we've tacked up properly and I got a perfect score for my tack today. These marks go towards presentation night at the end of the year. I hope I win something!

My first class today was rider class. This is

something I've been working on for a while with Sparkle. It's amazing how much easier it is to get it right on Tara though. The instructor kept commenting on how good I looked and how much I've improved. But I still have to work on my canter leads. Sometimes I'm on the right lead and sometimes not. We'll have to keep practicing those.

All through the morning, everyone was commenting on my new pony and saying how nice she is. The instructors were really happy to see me on such a good horse. I was having the best time!

When we did some sporting events in the afternoon, Tara was really quick and even managed to win the bounce pony. That was really cool! And when we did jumping, I wasn't nervous or worried at all. I'm not doing big jumps yet, but she is very willing and I already feel much more confident than I used to.

And to top it all off – Tara walked straight onto the float in the afternoon. Shelley's horse Millie still gets scared, but seeing Tara go straight on, made her feel safe I guess, then she walked on easily as well.

But poor Sparkle was left at home on her own in the paddock today. And she certainly didn't like it when Shelley and I took Tara and Millie out this morning. She wanted to come too and I was a bit worried about leaving her. Luckily though, the other girls' horses are in Ali's paddock, so she could still see them over the fence.

I think she would freak out if we left her completely by herself. It's amazing how quickly the horses have become so attached to each other. It's really beautiful to see.

I love my babies!

And I had the best day ever!!

Kate's friend…her first time on a horse!

Wednesday 19 June

I've been so busy! Having a new horse to ride and 9 puppies to help look after is really hectic. I also have a gymkhana coming up in a couple of weeks so I've been trying to ride Tara as much as possible to get ready for it. I'm sure we'll do well in the sporting but I'd love to win rider class – that would be really cool!

I'm glad that I have another day of pony club before the gymkhana so I can practice with the instructor some more. She is so helpful and she's taught me heaps! I've been working on Tara's canter leads and Mom seems to think that I'm usually on the right one now. A bit more practice and I think we'll be ready.

We were late getting home this afternoon though, because we had to stop in at the local newspaper office to get more newspaper for Sheba and her pups. Luckily they had stacks that they could give us – we're definitely going to need it!

The puppies are getting bigger and fatter and even cuter than ever. I didn't think they could get any more adorable but they actually are! But poor little Tina – she hasn't grown and we're really worried that she may not live. She still drags herself along and tries to get her share of milk. And we still have to make a space for her at feed times, or she'd never get fed. And we got some bad news today, the vet said that she'll probably have to be put down.

That is so sad! How can we have her put down? Poor Sheba! Imagine losing another one of her babies!

Sheba's pups are adorable. I'm glad there's healthy ones at least!

Friday 21 June

Tina died last night. It was so sad when we woke up and found her this morning especially when we saw Sheba licking her and gently prodding her with her paw. I started crying and Nate did too. We went out and buried her in the paddock. We found a special place under a tree and Nate made a little cross for her grave this afternoon after school.

Mom said that it was good we had to go to school because it would take our minds off it. I thought about it all day long though. I didn't want to concentrate on school and I felt really sad – I still do.

Thank goodness the other 8 puppies are so healthy and strong. We just have to really look after Sheba now. Feeding all those pups is really hard on her and she's started losing weight and looking exhausted. It's such a big job! Dad stocked up on extra special feed for her today to give her energy and put some weight back on. We'll have to feed her lots more than usual. I'm sure she'll enjoy that. She loves her food that's for sure.

At one of my parties a couple of years ago, we had a sausage sizzle and Dad left a huge plate of leftover sausages on the brick wall by the pool. Not many had been eaten because everyone was having too much fun in the pool. The mistake he made was that he hadn't thought about Sheba! She got to that plate and ate every single one of those sausages. There must have been 20-30 of them and she ate them ALL. She could barely walk afterwards and her stomach was HUGE!! We had to put her on a diet after that!

We're really lucky to have such a beautiful dog!

Sunday 23 June

I've spent this weekend, riding Tara around the big paddock – getting her fit and muscly and training her for the gymkhana as well. There's been no one around to ride with though. I don't know what all the other girls have been up to, but I've been on my own in the paddock – with my babies of course. But it's not the same as having a friend to ride with! I wish Nikita and Cappy were still agisting here.

I'm glad I've got the gymkhana to focus on and the puppies of course. They're sure keeping me busy! It's going to be so hard to sell them when they're old enough. Mom and Dad are thinking about keeping one. That would be really special if we could. Imagine that – having Sheba and one of her puppies to play with. That would be great for Sheba when we're all out at school and work each day. She does have our cat, Soxy at home with her but he just tends to sleep the whole time. Once we came home and found the 2 of them asleep together. Soxy was curled up on Sheba's bed right next to her. He couldn't have got closer if he'd tried. But the funny part was, that he was right in the middle of her comfy bed and there was no room for Sheba, so she was sleeping mainly on the floor. Soxy thinks he's the boss, I'm sure of it!

Saturday 6 July

I could not believe what happened today! The top part of my leg is now pure purple!!! I've never seen such a massive bruise before!

When I went into the paddock this afternoon to get Tara and tack her up, Millie came over and suddenly kicked out towards us. Something must have scared her or she didn't want me near Tara, because she just came over and kicked. I happened to be right in the line of fire and her hoof lashed into my thigh.

I could hear myself scream. It was really weird because it was like I was watching the whole thing happen. But it was actually really happening to me. And all I know is that I've never felt anything so painful before! I collapsed on the ground and couldn't stand up, the pain was that bad. I just had to lie down holding onto my thigh.

Mom came running over calling– Are you alright? Are you alright? She sounded really scared. This has happened to her once before as well, so she knows exactly what it's like.

Ali's horse, Charlie was grazing in our big paddock one time last year and Mom went to catch Sparkle for me. Then all of a sudden, Charlie kicked out at her and managed to get her right in the shin. I remember being so worried about Mom when that happened, because she screamed but then she couldn't talk. She just kind of keeled over, holding her leg.

And the worst part was that because it broke the skin and caused a cut, she ended up with blood poisoning. This is because there's so many germs in a horse paddock and the germs from Charlie's hoof got into Mom's bloodstream. She had to have about a week off work and almost had to go to hospital. Her foot swelled up so much, it looked like a football and she had to stay in bed with it elevated. Any time she wanted to stand and lower her leg, the pain was so incredible, she said it almost made her feel like passing out! It took a whole week before she could walk again and the doctor said that she was very lucky as it could've been extremely serious.

So when Mom saw me lying on the ground after being kicked by Millie, she started to panic. A kick from a horse can cause terrible injuries and we've heard of one girl who was kicked in the back and ended up in a wheelchair!

At first I couldn't talk. It reminded me of seeing Mom doing exactly the same thing when she was kicked. Then all I could think of was the gymkhana tomorrow! How am I going to be able to ride properly after this? I have to go to the gymkhana – it's my first one on Tara and I've been really, really looking forward to it!!!

Mom raced back to the house to get some ice and that helped a lot. After about 20 minutes with the ice on my leg, I told her that I was ready to ride. I had to train for the gymkhana tomorrow and there was no way I was going to let a horse kick stop me - even with a massive bruise on my thigh, the perfect shape of a horse shoe. I'm very lucky though that it's more to the side of my thigh because when I hopped in the saddle, I found that I don't actually put pressure on it when I sit. Otherwise I really don't think I'd be able to compete tomorrow. Shelley will be so upset when she hears. That Millie! She can be such a problem sometimes!! Mom's just relieved that all I've ended up with is a bruise and not a broken leg or much worse than that!

Then after my training session, I had to bathe Tara as well. It's been a full on afternoon, but I have to make sure she's looking shiny and clean. She's such a pretty pony, I'm sure I'll get a ribbon in best presented, especially if I also clean my tack really well tonight. And I'll get up early in the morning so I can braid her mane and tail. I'm getting much better at it now and it doesn't take me very long anymore. It'd be good if Mom could help, but she's hopeless at braiding. She even has trouble doing my plaits for school each day.

Anyway, I'm glad it was Nate's turn to clean up after the puppies tonight. I've got too many other things to do. But I had to write about what happened today while it's still fresh in my mind. I think the photo Mom took says it all though! I never want that to happen to me again, that's for sure!

I still can't believe that Millie kicked me!

Sunday 7 July

I was really excited this morning! It was tricky getting to sleep last night though because every time I rolled onto my right side where the bruise is, it woke me up. It does feel very, very sore if I bump it or even try to run around. But thank goodness, it's fine when I'm sitting still. Because I had an incredible day today – bruise and all!

We arrived at the gymkhana nice and early so I would have time to groom Tara, paint her hooves with hoof oil and braid her tail. I'm so glad I have Mom and Dad to help me!! I decided not to worry about her mane. I just did a small braid in her forelock and threaded some maroon and cream ribbon through it. Then when Mom went to fill Tara's water bucket, she bumped into Robin, who is one of the moms from pony club. Robin happened to be braiding the tail of her daughter's horse and when mom commented on what a beautiful job she was doing, she offered to braid Tara's tail as well. I couldn't believe my luck, because she's an expert at braiding and Tara's tail ended up looking so professional! It was much better than what I could have done, that's for sure! I then decided to do a checker pattern on her rump using a nit comb. I've seen other girls doing this and it looks really cool. Tara looked so beautiful when she was finally tacked up and ready. And I felt really proud!!

We went in the march past and our club came second overall – we're very lucky to have such nice uniforms that really stand out. Plus we all had such beautifully groomed horses as well! Then everyone went off into their separate age groups. First of all was best presented and I was thrilled because Tara got the blue ribbon. It was such a great start to the day! She really did look gorgeous though. And the extra time I spent cleaning my tack and boots last night obviously paid off.

It was perfect timing as well because Josh's mom, Tracey arrived just in time to see me win first place. She had told me she was going to try and come, so it was awesome to see that she could make it. I was using the brow band she made me as well. The pony club colors looked gorgeous across Tara's forehead and I know Tracey was pleased to see me using it. I told her that helped us to win – I think she liked that! But I know she was definitely happy to see that Tara is being well looked after.

The first event was bounce pony and Tracey said that Josh always did very well on her in this. I started to feel a bit nervous though because Tracey was watching. I tried to push her on and get her speed up, but she seemed a bit sluggish and I ended up coming 5th. It was great to get another ribbon, but I would have like to have done better – especially with Tracey there.

The next event was barrels and before I had my turn, Tracey gave me some tips that Josh always used when he was competing. She said that this really helped to get Tara going. Before my turn, I had to canter her around in a nearby space a few times to get her psyched up and ready to race. Then as I took off for my turn in the event, I had to give her a good tap with my crop and say – YAH!! YAH!! YAH!! And this worked brilliantly, because I WON!!

I was almost jumping for joy in the saddle! We'd won ribbons in every event so far and I already had 2 blues!

The next event for my age group was rider class. And I really started to get nervous as soon as I realised that! I've been working very hard for this event and I desperately wanted to do well. There were 14 girls in my age group and some really good riders – I remembered them from the last gymkhana. But then I saw who the judge was! It was Keith Lunn. He came as a special guest instructor to our pony club once and everyone was raving about how good he is. Just the sight of him made me even more nervous!

Anyway, because there were so many of us, we all had to do a few laps around the arena, following Keith's instructions while he watched us. Then he asked some people to leave. I was relieved when I realized that I was being asked to stay and continue. At that stage, there were 8 of us left, but obviously only 5 ribbons to be given out. First of all, we had to trot and then go into a canter. I knew that Tara had been on the right lead earlier, which was why we were given another turn. And I was concentrating really hard on making sure that she did that again. I was fairly confident that she was doing it right. At least, I really hoped so, anyway! Then, when he told us all to stop, we had to wait while he decided who should be given ribbons. He gave the white to a girl on a pretty grey mare and then handed the yellow to the girl beside her. After that he headed back up the line towards me and I was sure he was going to hand me the green but he walked straight past. I started to feel sick then, because there were only 2nd and 1st place ribbons to go. All I could think was – is it possible that I could've come 2nd? But then he walked back past me and handed it to a girl on a beautiful chestnut gelding that looked like he belonged in the show ring. My heart sank! It was all I'd been looking forward to and the one ribbon I really wanted to take home – even a white or yellow one for this event would have made me happy!

But then all of a sudden, he was handing the blue to me! I just couldn't believe it was happening! Mom said later that the smile on my face was priceless. She said that she'd been feeling sick with nerves just watching me – and she wasn't even the one riding. But I guess she knew how much it meant and how hard I've been working! Bruise and all – I managed to actually win rider class. I was over the moon!

The mother of the girl who came 5th even congratulated me which was really nice and commented on how lovely my new pony is. She said that she remembered me from the last gymkhana when I was riding Sparkle. The girl who came 3rd congratulated me as well. She was in my group last time and we've kind of become friends. Mom, Dad and Tracey were all raving on about it. I felt so proud!! I don't think I'll ever forget that moment!!!

I then took Tara over to the trailer for a well-deserved lunch break. Just as I started to untack her, we heard on the loud speakers that the Champion Rider event was being held and that all rider class winners had to go to the show ring. This was such a shock because I certainly hadn't been expecting to have to do this. So then I had to quickly get my saddle and bridle back on Tara and race back over to the show ring.

Oh my gosh! I thought I was nervous for rider class but this sure did beat that a hundred times over. I had so many butterflies going around in my stomach that I could hardly ride properly! The ring was full of huge horses and because I'm in one of the younger age groups, there were heaps of older riders and even some ladies in the ring with me as well. And their horses looked spectacular! It was so scary! Even Mom said afterwards that it looked really intimidating.

Just as we all transitioned to a canter, the judge asked us to hand gallop and I had no idea what she was talking about! So all I could do was try to copy the others.

Thank goodness Tracey had left by then because I was really glad she wasn't watching – that would've been even more embarrassing! I'm going to have to ask about the hand gallop when I go to pony club next week – just in case I'm ever asked to do it again. Anyway, I certainly wasn't expecting a ribbon in that event and I was kind of relieved to be asked to leave the ring. It was good to get out of there!

But then just as we managed to sit down and have a rest and some lunch, we heard the call that the afternoon program was beginning. So I had to quickly finish eating, get Tara tacked up again and race over to the jumping ring.

When I got there though, the girls had just finished walking the course with the judge, so I missed out on that. I simply had to line up with the other riders and wait for my turn. When I was called in to start, I headed straight for the first jump and cleared it. That really helped me to feel confident about the rest of them. I then managed to get around the course and only knocked one jump off. Dad said that Tara just clipped it with her hoof, which was a shame as she had pretty much cleared it easily. I really enjoyed that event and felt I'd done very well, but just as I was heading out of the ring, the judge called me over to tell me I was disqualified. I couldn't believe what I was hearing! How could I be disqualified? She told me that I hadn't gone through the start gate and that caused instant disqualification. I felt like crying! It wasn't fair! I told her that I hadn't been able to walk the course and wasn't told about it. But she said there was nothing she could do and I had to leave the ring.

So I just had to stand and watch the rest of the riders compete and then be given their ribbons at the end. I was so upset! I couldn't believe that had happened to me. And I still feel really upset thinking about it even now! Mom said, that at least I've learnt what to do and that I'll never make that mistake again. That doesn't help much though. It was really disappointing!!!!

After that it was time for the mystery event which Tara did not like at all! Sparkle was one of the few horses that would easily walk through all the scary bits and pieces, but I couldn't even get Tara over the plastic that was laid on the ground at the start. Let alone the streamers they had hanging down. There was no way she was going to go through those! Dad suggested that we put some up in the paddock to get her used to them, so she's not so frightened. We might try and do that this week then I can start practicing on her. I should probably put plastic down for her to walk over as well. It's amazing what horses are scared of. They're such big animals but they really are huge scaredy cats. Most of them, anyway!

But regardless of the jumping and mystery events, I still came home with 5 ribbons overall which is such a great result and I even got a pink one. I'd had my eye on those all day but only some judges were giving them out, kind of like an encouragement award. And I ended up getting a pink for flags which is an event I've never done before. So that was really cool.

Then I got the surprise of my life, because at the presentation at the very end of the day, I was given a trophy for coming 4th in my age group overall. I couldn't believe it when my name was announced. That really made up for being disqualified for jumping. I was so happy – it was such a fantastic end to the day!!

What a wonderful dream pony I have. She is just

awesome to ride and to compete on. She didn't do anything naughty at all – oh, except refuse to go in the Mystery event. But that's okay – we'll just work on that one.

I gave her some extra feed tonight when we got home. She certainly deserved it! And she didn't even seem tired – I really think she could have kept on going.

I know that I'll sleep well tonight though. I'm exhausted!

Monday 8 July

This morning at school, Miss Johnson took us down to the oval for our morning run. She's a fitness freak and wants us all to get really fit, like her. She says it also helps us to learn better when we go back to class and is a really great way to start the day. I don't usually mind too much, because I want to get fit. But I just knew that it would hurt because of my bruise!

So when I told her that I couldn't run today because I have a bruise, she just laughed at me and told me to get going. When I told my best friend Tina, she said – You have to show her! She doesn't understand! – Tina was in shock when I showed her earlier this morning. Of course she was tempted to poke at it and that really did hurt. Anyway, the thought of having to run around the oval 3 times was just too much, so I decided to pull up the leg of my shorts so Miss Johnson could see what I was talking about.

It was actually really funny to watch her jaw drop! She said – OH MY GOSH!!!! You really DO have a bruise!!!!! How on earth did you do that?

When I explained what had happened, she quickly told me I'd better go and sit down. So at

172

least it got me out of running, I guess!

Anyway, I've been thinking about Tara and the mystery event and Dad said that he has some old black plastic that I can use. So we're going to cut it up and hang it off one of the branches of the big tree in the paddock. I'm looking forward to seeing what she thinks of that!

Now I need to go and put some fresh newspaper down for the pups. They're definitely getting bigger and noisier. I can even hear them from my room. At least we all get to cuddle them on our laps now while we're watching TV at night. And they are so cuddly!!

Aren't they beautiful!!

Thursday 11 July

Well, we're going to need lots of practice walking Tara through the streamers. She's not keen on them at all and insisted on just going around when we tried her this afternoon. We're just going to leave them attached to the tree for now and hopefully she'll get used to them eventually.

She wasn't too bad with the plastic on the ground though. It took a bit of patience, but in the end, I got her to walk over it.

I just love her!!!

Sunday 21 July

I don't think anything can compare to doing what we did today!!!

Jo and Nikita invited me to go with them to the lake that's not too far from our house. They go riding there all the time and Nikita's told me how much fun it is to ride horses in water. She said the horses love it too. It was so nice that Nikita asked me to come along. I haven't seen her since they moved their horses out of our front paddock and I've really been missing her.

So we got up early and met them down at the lake. Mom and Dad helped me unload Tara and tack her up then they arranged to meet us back at the same spot later in the morning. I had my favorite pink horsey T shirt on and I was so excited!

We had to go along a trail first which led to the lake. And, oh my goodness. Words can't describe how beautiful it looked at 6:30 this morning!!! The sun was rising over the crystal, clear water which was just like a sheet of glass! It was the most perfect day and one of the most beautiful views I've ever seen!

The water was only about a foot deep along the edge and the horses were able to splash around in it. Because it was quite shallow, it wasn't a struggle for them to move through it. This must have felt really good because they absolutely loved it! Then we started cantering, their hooves splashing up water all around me. It was definitely the best feeling in the whole world! It felt like I was flying!

But then I happened to look down in the water and screamed. Tara had almost stepped on a sting ray that was swimming past us. That was freaky!

After a while, we went back through the bush and onto a jumping track where some of the trails had little logs that we could jump over. So we cantered through and it was SO much fun. At the end of the track, we had to keep them moving so the lactic acid didn't build up in their joints after all the cantering and jumping.

Then we slowed down to a walk and passed a paddock where a donkey was grazing. It was quite funny, because Tara became startled when she saw it. It was like she was saying – What's that scary thing?? It really made me laugh. She's such a cutie!

When we headed back through the water, I ended up being in the lead alongside Jo. I asked if we could canter and then the horses started racing each other. I called out to Jo - Can we gallop? And it was the most magical feeling in the entire world. The water was so clean and clear, we could even see the sand at the bottom.

I don't think I've ever experienced the feeling I had today. Galloping through that lake is the highlight of my life so far! It was AMAZING!!!

I want to go again tomorrow!!!!

Next time I want to take our horses swimming – not where there's any stingrays though!

Sunday 28 July

It was pouring with rain again this morning so pony club was cancelled. There's been rain on and off all week but I was hoping that it would stop for today. I was really looking forward to going. At least the rain stopped this afternoon though, so I got to have a ride in the small paddock at least – it tends to stay drier than our big paddock, which is lucky.

Tara didn't seem to be herself today. Maybe the bad weather is making her cranky. The paddock was pretty wet anyway, so I only had a short ride.

I hope that it's fine next Sunday because Pony Club has been rescheduled for then.

I'll have to pray for good weather!

Friday 1 August

Finally the sun came out today! I was so glad because today is Tara and Sparkle's birthday. Well, I don't actually know which day they were born exactly, but every horse has their birthday on 1 August. Here in Australia, anyway. Apparently in the Northern hemisphere it's on 1 January. I don't know why it can't be the same all over the world!

So, we celebrated my babies birthdays this afternoon when I got home from school. I made them 2 special horsey cakes with all their favorites. I included some oats and chaff, 2 large grated carrots, some chopped up apple and banana (Sparkle's favourite) and then added some molasses and honey to help bind it all together and as an extra sweet treat. Then I put them on 2 separate plates and even put candles on top. Mom, Dad, Nate and I all sang happy birthday and I blew out the candles for them.

Tara and Sparkle were so good. The candles didn't bother them at all. I think they were too interested in what was on the plate to be worried about candles. They certainly enjoyed their treat, that's for sure!

Sunday 3 August

Something happened at pony club today that I was not expecting. I was doing rider class and I'd just finished telling my favorite instructor, Kylie, that I had won first place in the gymkhana a couple of weeks ago. And then Tara started to pig root. I've seen horses do this before, but I've never experienced it myself. It gave me a bit of a fright at first but I kept on riding. Then she did it again – and again – and again! I started to get scared and Kylie told me to be firm with her and use a gruff voice to tell her to stop. But she just kept doing it and I had to hop off. I didn't know what was wrong! All I did know was that she was really scaring me!

Kylie could see how upset I was and decided to hop on her herself. But Tara just kept pig rooting and wouldn't stop. She told me that Tara was probably in season and being a moody mare and that I shouldn't do the class. That was really upsetting because I just had to stand and watch. I didn't know why Tara was behaving like that!

One of the moms told me that if she is in season it would explain her behavior. She said that there is actually a vaccination that can be given to prevent this and suggested we speak to the vet. Mom and I didn't like the sound of that, but think we might try the herbal medicine that she said is also available for moody mares. I guess this is another reason why geldings are so popular!

After the class finished, one of the other girls, Jackie, who's a pretty experienced rider, hopped on Tara and took her for a ride. She did a few pig roots but Jackie was really firm with her, using her voice and some taps of her crop. This made Tara settle right down and behave. Jackie said that I'm going to have to learn to do the same thing if Tara keeps behaving like this and let her know that I'm the boss.

I went to my next class and when Tara tried it again, I was able to manage her a lot better. But then in the afternoon classes, she just kept pigrooting and I wasn't able to do much riding at all. Maybe she's just trying to be in control or maybe she's in season. Or, maybe it's a combination of both.

Mom rang Tracey tonight to tell her what had happened and she said that if Tara ever misbehaved with Josh, that he would just be firm with her and not put up with it. But she said that it didn't happen very much and wasn't really too much of a problem. It seems to be a lot worse when I'm riding her though! And I wonder why?

We want to get on top of this as soon as possible, so Mom and Dad have decided to arrange for a horse trainer to come to our house to work with her. She's instructed at pony club before and apparently is really good with problem horses.

But Tara can't possibly be a problem horse! I haven't had her very long and she's my dream pony!! I hope that the trainer can come soon though. I want my dream pony back!!!

One of the instructors at pony club

Wednesday 6 August

I don't know what to do! I've just had the worst news and I'm actually freaking out right now!! I've spent most of the afternoon in my room. And I feel sick with worry.

The horse trainer came today. And I can't believe what she told us!!!

First of all we tacked Tara up and then Janice the trainer, checked out her saddle to make sure it was sitting correctly on her back. She didn't really find any problems there, so next she began to longe her. To begin with, Tara was cooperating, but then she suddenly started to pig root. And she wouldn't stop! She got so bad that she actually almost looked dangerous! I was really scared! But Janice was really firm with her and managed to calm her down so she could hop on. Within minutes though, she hopped off again. She said that she didn't want to risk riding her because she was being so hard to handle. I didn't really blame her! There was no way I was going to get on her while she was like that, that's for sure!

I asked Janice - Why is she suddenly behaving like this?

I just couldn't understand it. But it was her answer that shocked me even more than Tara's behavior!

"This horse is a nightmare! You need to get rid of her!"

That is what she told me. I could not believe what I was hearing! How could she say that about my dream pony? It just doesn't make sense! She's been absolutely perfect until now. There must be a reason why she's behaving this way.

Janice said that there's a possibility she's been drugged by her previous owners so they could sell her. She said that the calming effects can last a few months, then the new owners are stuck with the psycho horse that they've bought.

I just know that Tracey wouldn't do something like this! And Mom and Dad agree. There's no way that this could have happened to Tara. Tracey loves her and was genuinely upset to be selling her.

But Janice is adamant that we've bought a real problem horse in Tara. And says that she can try to work with her and get her to a stage where she can be sold.

When I got back to the house this afternoon, I just ran into my room and started to cry. And I've been here ever since. This can't be happening. Tara is my dream pony. We've been through so many problems with Sparkle, I just wanted a pony that I can enjoy and have fun on.

What am I going to do?

If we have to sell her, there's no way Mom and Dad will buy me another horse! I know them – they'll just say that's it! No more!! It's all too hard and maybe you're better off without a horse at all.

But what about Tara? What's going to happen to her? Janice even said that horses like her often end up at the doggers. That's where they take horses and kill them for dog meat.

I can't let this happen. There has to be more to it. Why would she suddenly start to behave like this? It just doesn't make any sense!

We can't just give up on her! We just can't!!!!

PLEASE SAVE MY BABY!!!!

Book 4

Pony Pals

Thursday 7 August

I didn't sleep at all last night! All I did was toss and turn, worrying about my baby! What's going to happen to her? And why is she like this in the first place! It just doesn't make any sense. How can my dream pony suddenly become my worst nightmare?

She was so scary in the paddock yesterday, when Janice was longeing her. I can't believe she was actually willing to hop on Tara after seeing how crazy she was behaving!

I'm so relieved that Mom and Dad disagree with Janice though! They can't understand it either but definitely don't think Tara's been drugged. Mom said that she's going to talk to some people from pony club who might be able to help. Thank goodness for that! I was so worried about how they'd react to all of this. Surely now we can find someone to help her! We have to find the cause, we just have to!

And then we have to get her back to the way she was.

But is that going to be possible??

Friday 8 August

Last night, Mom called one of the parents from pony club. A little while ago, he told her about a man who is not only a very experienced horse trainer but also a horse healer. Apparently he worked wonders with their daughter's pony, Rocco who was behaving really badly and wasn't able to be ridden. So Mom decided to get his details so she could ask him about Tara. Now he's coming over on Sunday afternoon to have a look at her.

I'm so glad he can come and I hope he can help!!!

Saturday 9 August

Now more drama! As if we haven't got enough to worry about...

This afternoon, we let Sheba's pups out for a big run on the acre or so of grass that we have down by the pool. They absolutely love it when they're able to do this. Their little ears flap up and down and they all have the biggest smiles on their faces. It literally looks like they're grinning from ear to ear! 8 little golden retriever puppies bouncing around is the cutest thing you've ever seen!!

It's tricky though because they each run in different directions and we have to keep doing a head count to make sure we have them all.

Anyway, tonight Dad found a tick on Elvis. Out of all the pups, he's my favorite! It was just lucky that Dad discovered it when he was cuddling him on the lounge. We've made a habit of doing this every night while we're watching TV. Each of us chooses one of the pups to cuddle and play with. We try to give them all a turn because they've become so cute and so cuddly and are really, really affectionate. They actually are totally irresistible!

Usually when we're holding them, I have Elvis – because he is my favorite. But for some reason, Dad ended up with him tonight. This is really lucky because I might not have found the tick and by tomorrow, it could have been too late.

Dad didn't want to risk him getting really sick, so he's taken him to the afterhours vet to be checked over. He's one of the 5 that have already been sold and the new owners are all coming to collect them next weekend. I hope he's going to be ok!

And besides that, he really is my favorite. He's very fat and cuddly - I just adore him. When we were trying to think of names for them all, Dad came up with Elvis (that's because he's a huge Elvis Presley fan) – and it suits this little puppy so much!

It's going to be really sad when they're all sold. And especially when Elvis goes. Poor Sheba! I wonder how she's going to cope?

At least we'll still have 3 pups left – for a little while at least. They're the ones that aren't sold yet. But Mom and Dad have decided not to keep any – which is such a shame! They think we've got enough going on as it is – especially with 2 horses in the paddock and all the trouble we're having with Tara.

I'd still love to keep one though. And if I could…I would keep Elvis.

Sunday 10 August

The horse trainer and healer arrived this afternoon. His name is Dieter and he's from Switzerland. Apparently, he's worked with horses all through Europe - so he certainly must be experienced!

When he first saw Tara, he commented on what a beautiful horse she is! This instantly made me feel a lot better. He said that his favorite type of riding is endurance and that he'd love to take her on an endurance ride as he could tell that she'd be perfect for this. I told him that other people have mentioned the same thing to me before.

He then started to check her over. He was really gentle and kind, talking softly to her the whole time. I could see that she was unsure at first, but he has such a lovely way with horses, that she soon started to relax.

I was feeling very tense though – I was really worried about what he would find.

Gradually, he moved his hands firmly but carefully across her back, feeling in every area for anything unusual. Janice did this briefly when she was checking her over, but seemed to think that she was fine.

That certainly wasn't what Dieter thought

though! He could tell by the way Tara was reacting when he pressed firmly on certain parts of her back that she is very, very sore. He told us that she even has tears in the muscles across the sides of her upper back! He then said that he isn't surprised at all that she's behaving so badly – because of course she must be in a lot of pain, especially when she's being ridden.

I couldn't believe what he was telling me! I saw Tara flinch and toss her head as well as push her ears right back when he pressed on certain areas. So it was really obvious that what he was saying was true. How could Janice, an experienced horse person and trainer, not pick that up? And then tell us that Tara isn't worth anything and should go to the doggers!!!!

Dieter then wanted to see my saddle. It was hanging up in the shed with all my other tack and as soon as I showed it to him, he said – This is the cause of the problem!!

He explained that it's completely unsuitable for Tara and is what has actually caused the tears and sore muscles in her back.

This was such a shock! My beautiful shiny saddle that still looks almost brand new has caused my dream pony to be in so much pain. So much pain that she's actually become a nightmare horse!

I certainly wasn't expecting this. And I feel terrible about it.

No one has picked this up before – not at pony club or anywhere. I can't believe that by putting that saddle on Tara and riding her, I've put her in so much pain. How could I have done this?

Dieter told me that my Wintec has to go. I can't use it on her ever again. And he says that the perfect style saddle for Tara's shaped back is a Stuben. These saddles come from Switzerland and he said that they're his favorite brand of saddle. The best quality and comfort for both horses and their riders.

So that now obviously means a new saddle for Tara. I really wasn't sure what Mom would say about this because saddles are really expensive. But she just wanted to know where we could get one and how much it would be. I was so relieved until he told us what they do cost – thousands of dollars. For a saddle!! All I could think was, how on earth can we afford one of those?

But thank goodness he's pretty sure we'll be able to find a good quality second hand one on the internet. And Mom said that we can sell my Wintec. So that'll help to pay for it.

Then it was time for him to treat Tara's condition and I got another surprise. He pulled out a pouch of needles and said that he's going to use acupuncture on her. Acupuncture on a horse! Mom and Dad use natural therapies all the time and we've all had acupuncture ourselves before, but I did not know that it's a treatment that can be used for horses!

Mom was so impressed with him. He really seems to know what he's talking about. I wasn't sure how Tara would cope with needles in her back though. But because he is so caring and gentle, she was actually fine. He talked to her the whole time in a really soothing voice, while I stood holding her lead rope. I stroked her forehead and whispered in her ear to comfort her and I know that helped a lot as well.

Dieter said that it'll be a few weeks and a few more treatments, before Tara will be fit to ride again but then she should be absolutely fine. Mom has complete faith in him. She thinks he's amazing!! We are very lucky to have found someone who is this experienced and knows so much.

Luckily my Wintec is in really good condition. We should be able to sell it fairly easily as they're quite popular.

And hopefully, I'll get enough money so it will pay for the new Stuben. Dieter said that we should be able to find something without too much trouble as they're a fairly common saddle worldwide.

I certainly hope so! I miss riding Tara already.
But the main thing is, I just know that my baby
will be ok now and I'm going to have my dream
horse back!!

And to think that Janice was ready to send her
away for dog meat! I can feel my heart race
when I even think about the possibility of that
happening. How could anyone do this to their
pony??? Mom can't believe we actually paid
Janice to come and work with Tara and then tell
us what she did!

Thank goodness we persevered!!!

Tara's going to be ok! I just know it!!!

Monday 11 August

Well it's not been as easy as we thought to find a Stuben that's the right size for me and also for Tara. Mom's been searching online but hasn't come up with anything yet. I hope that Dieter is luckier! He's searching too and said that he'll call and let us know how he does.

On Wednesday afternoon, he's coming back to check on Tara and give her more acupuncture. Hopefully by then, he'll have found me a saddle.

And Elvis came home today. The vet wanted to keep him for 2 nights so he could keep an eye on him to make sure he's ok – which he is. Thank goodness! We're really lucky though. Because he's only 9 weeks old, he could have become very sick. Now we have to keep him quiet for the rest of the week, so he can recover. The poor little thing. He's normally really boisterous – I could tell that it's taken its toll on him. We're probably going to have to keep him for an extra week now to make sure he's ok before leaving his mom.

But I don't mind that at all!!

Wednesday 13 August

Dieter came this afternoon and treated Tara again. The good news is that she already seems to be healing nicely and he's sure that she'll be back to normal within a couple of weeks. This is awesome because there's a pony club camp coming up in the school holidays next month that I desperately want to go to. And Dieter said that as long as I can find the right saddle, Tara will definitely be fine for that!

He also brought a saddle with him today, to see whether it might be the right size. He just held it above her back to get an idea if it might fit but it was too big. It also wasn't a Stuben so it probably wasn't ideal anyway. But he just thought that he would try it.

This is because he's had no luck finding a Stuben online so far.

I haven't given up though! I'm sure the right saddle is going to come along and I'll be riding my beautiful dream pony again before I know it!

Saturday 16 August

I knew everything would work out!!!

Dieter came again today to give Tara another treatment of acupuncture. Afterwards he said that she probably won't need anymore, just another week or so of rest and she should be healed enough for me to ride her.

And he's managed to find me a Stuben! He was able to bring it on loan from the local saddlery so that we can see if it's the right size. And it is! He said he couldn't believe it when he walked in there yesterday afternoon and there it was. I'm so happy!

It's an old one but it's pure leather and in really good condition. Apparently these types of saddles last forever! It's going to be hard to give up my beautiful new saddle for an old looking one, but if it means I can ride again, then that's all that matters really. The only thing is, it'll be more work to keep it clean. My Wintec is vinyl and only needs to be wiped over with a damp cloth whereas leather saddles have to be oiled and cleaned regularly to keep them in good condition.

But I don't care, as long as I can ride, that's all that matters!

I'm so happy!!

Sunday 17 August

4 of Sheba's pups went to new homes today. It was really sad to see them go! They really are just like cuddly teddy bears – big balls of fluff and so cute!!!!

It reminds me of when Sheba was a puppy and how adorable she was then. Golden retriever pups have to be the cutest puppies ever. I think so anyway!!

At least we still have 5 left for now. And we still have Elvis – for another week that is.

I think I'll go and give them all a big cuddle before I go to sleep.

Saturday 23 August

Elvis left today. I'm so glad we were able to have an extra week with him before he went. 2 other puppies were collected as well. Dad found homes for them during the week.

It was very sad to say goodbye. I especially didn't want Elvis to go! I'm going to miss him so much.

The good news is that Mom and Dad have the phone numbers of all the people who bought the puppies, so we can get together with most of them again. At least the ones that live in our local area, anyway. One was actually flown interstate. The people who bought her had her collected by a courier and taken to the airport. We were so relieved to get a phone call to tell us that she'd arrived safely and was actually ok. What a scary trip for a little puppy on her own!

I wonder if Sheba will remember her babies when we do see them next?

Now we only have Brian left. He's the escape artist and Dad's favorite. We don't have a home for him yet. So maybe we'll end up being able to keep him after all.

That would be just awesome!!!

Wednesday 28 August

I'm over the moon!!!!

I rode Tara this afternoon and she was perfect! I only walked and trotted her. I didn't do anything too strenuous but she seems absolutely fine and didn't put her ears back once. In fact, she seemed really happy to be ridden again.

I was hoping to ride her last weekend but when Dieter came to check her over he said that she really needed another few days. Anyway, it was worth the wait, because today, she was just beautiful to ride.

This afternoon Dieter longed her for a while first, to help get rid of any excess energy before I hopped on. He showed me how to do this properly and said I should always longe her before riding. Anyway, by the time I rode her, she was calm and absolutely wonderful. Just like when I rode her for the very first time.

And the other good news is that my Stuben saddle seems to be perfect. It's really, really comfy as well. That's probably because it's so worn in. I do miss my beautiful Wintec though. It looked very pretty on Tara and all the other girls have the nicest new saddles as well. Now I'm going to turn up to pony club with a really old looking one. Dad bought some leather conditioner especially for saddles today, so hopefully that will help.

But at least I have my dream pony back!!! I'm SOOOO glad!!!

Saturday 31 August

Pony Club is tomorrow and Shelley's coming too. We bathed the horses this afternoon so they'll look beautiful for line up in the morning. I bathed Sparkle as well and I think she really enjoyed the attention! I've been so busy with Tara that I know I've been neglecting Sparkle lately. I do still love her though and I always will. She'll always be my baby!

I can't wait for tomorrow.

It's going to be SO much fun!!!

Sunday 1 September

Tara was absolutely awesome today – back to her usual beautiful self.

She did absolutely everything right. She was perfect during rider class and didn't pig root even once. All day long, she was just lovely. And jumping class this afternoon was really fun! I felt so confident on her and she loved it just as much as me, I could tell. I'm going to start practicing higher jumps, I think. I'm sure she'll be fine and I feel completely ready as well.

Everyone was really happy to see us there and pleased to see Tara being so well-behaved. I even had a couple of people ask me where I got her as they think she's such a lovely horse. One mom told me I'm very lucky to have found her and that I should do really well on her.

I can't wait until pony club camp in a few weeks. That's going to be the coolest thing ever! And there's even going to be a gymkhana on the last day. I can't wait for that!!

There are only a few girls from my pony club going and they're all camping together. But I'm going to camp with Nikita and her mom. We get to stay there for the whole week with our horses. It's going to be so cool.

I feel a bit funny not staying with the girls from

my pony club but Nikita and I have become good friends and we definitely want to be together. I am really excited about it. It's going to be awesome!

Today was such a great day but there was just one problem.

I was embarrassed about my saddle.

I saw a few girls looking at it and a couple of them asked me what happened to my Wintec. I explained but they didn't say very much. I could tell that they weren't impressed with the Stuben. That's because it's so old. Even though I've cleaned and polished it and that has made a big improvement, it still looks old. And almost everyone has new saddles.

It's kind of embarrassing to have such an old one – especially after being used to one that is brand new and so easy to keep clean!

I told Mom that I want to look for a new Stuben and she told me to stop sounding so spoilt! She said – Just be grateful that you have a saddle at all and that you can actually ride Tara again.

She wasn't happy with me at all.

I know she's right, but everyone has a new saddle and I want one too!

The Stuben is really comfy and definitely does

seem to suit Tara. But I miss my Wintec and I can't help it.

And to make matters worse, Cammie from across the road came home with a brand new saddle today. Her dad, Jim found it for her online. They're normally really expensive but he managed to get it for a really good price. Then I had to show her my new saddle. How embarrassing.

Maybe I can somehow save up and buy one myself. If I look online, I might even find one for a good price like Jim did.

You never know!

Wednesday 4 September

Dad found new owners for Brian and they're coming to collect him on Saturday. I'm really sad because he's the very last of Sheba's pups.

I was desperately hoping that we might be allowed to keep him. But after Elvis got a tick, and we came close to losing him, Mom and Dad said that Brian definitely has to go.

Sheba's immune to ticks now, which is great. Although, we did nearly lose her when she was about 6 months old. She got a tick and almost died. It was terrible. It took her a long time to build up her immunity and we had to check her constantly. Even with a tick collar and pills that are supposed to prevent ticks, she still managed to get them. And it's really hard to find ticks on a golden retriever, that's for sure. They have so much hair, that it's almost impossible.

Anyway, Mom and Dad didn't want to have to go through all that with Brian as well. They think one dog is enough. And also, Brian is an escape artist. He is so clever! We think he's the smartest dog of the whole litter. No matter what we do, he manages to find a way to get out of his enclosure. He's so inquisitive and curious and we've managed to start training him to do tricks already. He really does seem very intelligent. Even if he is hard work!

It's going to be the saddest thing to see him go on Saturday.

They were all so adorable as little babies!!! ☺

Saturday 7 September

Brian's gone.

And it was really hard to say goodbye!

Mom invited the new owners inside for a cup of tea. I'm sure it was just so she could keep Brian a little bit longer. We all took turns at nursing him on our laps in front of the TV last night. He's so big and fat and cuddly. And Mom didn't even care that he got his hair all over our red lounge. We usually have to avoid this or Mom freaks out.

She even insisted on carrying him downstairs to the new owner's car. We always carry the pups up and down the stairs. This is necessary until they're about 6 months of age, because it can be very bad for their hips while they're growing. Retrievers are prone to hip problems when they're older and you really need to take care while they're young.

I almost didn't think Mom was going to let them take him in the end. I think they probably felt the same way and were even getting a bit worried. We've all grown so attached to him – especially because he's the last one. It really was the saddest thing to say goodbye.

The one I feel most sorry for though, is Sheba!!!! Imagine how she must feel to see her puppies go. It seems really cruel to take all her babies off her.

It'd be like Sparkle or Tara being taken off me. I just know I wouldn't cope with that!!!

Poor Sheba!

Sunday 15 September

Nikita rang me tonight. She's so excited because she got a new horse today. He's a quarter horse called Darcy. That sounds like such a cheeky name. I wonder if he has the personality to go with it. She said that he's really beautiful – which I'm sure he is.

She's been looking for a new horse for a while now, because she's outgrown Cappy. He's just become way too small for her - she really did need a bigger horse.

And now she's just like me with Sparkle – she's going to try to convince her parents to let her keep Cappy as well as have Darcy.

Nikita and I are so much alike. No wonder we get on really well.

It's perfect because she has Darcy just in time for pony club camp. And there's one full week still to go so they can get used to each other.

I can't wait to meet him!

Thursday 19 September

I rode with Shelley today in the big paddock. We've been riding together a lot lately, along with Ali, Cammie and Grace when they're around. It's really fun having them all to ride with. I've been working on getting Tara really fit, so she'll be ready for camp next week. It's come up really quickly and I'm so excited about it.

All the girls wish they could go too. Shelley probably could go, but she doesn't have any friends her age who are going. I'm very lucky to be going with Nikita – we're going to have the best time!

It really can't come quickly enough!

Friday 20 September

FINALLY it's the school holidays and now there's only 2 more days until camp!

I'll have to go to bed early on Sunday night but I have so much to do to get ready before then. We want to get there really early to get a good camping spot and a good stall for the horses. At least I have the weekend to get organized. And it's great that we only live 20 minutes away. So it's easy for Mom or Dad to come each day to watch. They'll also be able to bring anything I need. They didn't want to camp over because that would be way too boring for Nate. He'll just want to go surfing in the holidays, not be at a pony club camp. But I'm going to have the best time. Especially camping with Nikita and Jo.

I CAN'T WAIT!!!!

Saturday 28 September

Oh my gosh!!!!!!!!!!!! I've just had the best week of my entire life!!!!!!!!!

I was so tired when I got home yesterday afternoon though. There was no way I could stay awake long enough to write anything. And now I can't believe that it's all over.

But the funny thing is, I think Tara could have just kept on going. The other horses all seemed worn out, but she still had so much energy. She definitely is an endurance horse, that's for sure.

I'm very lucky to have her and that's probably why I did so well in the gymkhana yesterday. Although, I'm sure I would have done well on her regardless of what condition the other horses were in. She's such a great pony!

But then, I should really start from the beginning. And there's so much to tell…

Of course, Nikita and I were really excited on the first day. We arrived at around the same time and met at the stables. This was our first priority because we were hoping to get stalls next to each other.

When I saw Darcy, I could see why Nikita had bought him – he is a really lovely horse. And he does seem quite cheeky - the name Darcy is perfect for him.

Then I saw the stables. And I thought I was in heaven. Actually, what I really thought was that I was in The Saddle Club. The movie, I mean! The stables were beautiful!!! They were indoor and really big and lovely – exactly like in The Saddle Club. I was even more excited than ever.

But then I found out that sections had been allocated to each pony club and this meant I'd have to keep Tara in a completely different area to Darcy. I instantly felt devastated. This was really disappointing. One of the moms must have heard us talking though, because out of the blue, she told us that her friend's daughter had cancelled at the last minute and that I could have her stall if I wanted it. And would you believe, it was the stall right next to Darcy!!

It was such a great start to the week!

Nikita's mom, Jo got her horse settled and then went off to reserve a good camping spot while we tacked up ready for our first class. We tacked up Jo's horse, as well, so he'd be ready for her when she came back. Luckily Mom was there to help us because we were rushing to be ready on time.

The program included 3 classes per day – a jumping class, a flatwork class and a theory class. And we were put into groups according to the jumping heights that we had chosen to focus on. Because it was our first camp, Jo advised us beforehand to go for smaller sized jumps so we wouldn't be pressured and could focus more on technique. That way we'd also probably enjoy it more. And it was the best idea, because it ended up being the most fun class of all.

Jo went off to her flatwork class and Nikita and I headed down to the jumping arena, as we had jumping first. I was really excited but I was also nervous and felt glad that I was with Nikita. There were 10 other girls in our group as well as us. None were from my pony club but there was one girl from Nikita's, called Jaz. Nikita introduced me to her. Although they weren't good friends, they had got to know each other a little this year.

Straight away I really liked Jaz. She seemed so nice and as soon as she said hello and smiled, I had the feeling that we'd all get along really well. She has a 13.2 hand grey called Jasper. And he is so gorgeous!

It turned out that our jumping instructor was John Jamieson, whom we all know as he's instructed at our pony clubs before. It was great to have him because he's such an awesome instructor.

John is actually in a movie. It's an Australian

movie called, The Man from Snowy River and he's one of the horsemen. Mom said that it was really popular when it first came out – I must remember to ask if we can hire it so we can look out for him…plus I'd love to see it.

In our jumping class, John first of all set up some low jumps and wanted us to do a few exercises with the horses. He placed a pole on the ground one stride before the jump to teach the horses to get their timing right. We did this a few times and Tara timed each jump absolutely perfectly every single time! I didn't think much of it, but when I looked at some of the other riders I could see that they were having trouble getting their horses to do it correctly.

When John stopped us to talk about what we'd been doing, he commented that Tara was the best horse. He said that she's so well-trained and obedient and had done it every time without fault. He then asked to use me as an example so Tara and I could show the other girls how it should be done. I overheard Jaz say to her dad, who was watching, - I want a horse like Tara!

I felt *SO* proud!!

After the class finished, it was time for lunch. We took the horses back to their stalls, untacked them and fed them each a biscuit of hay. Then Jo suggested we walk them over to a lovely shaded, grassy area on a hill nearby that she had found. This way we could watch them graze while we ate our lunch. We thought this was a great idea and asked Jaz if she wanted to come too.

We decided to do this every day at lunch time. We just sat on that hill chatting all about horses while our babies grazed on the green grass. We did this every morning and evening as well. Just to get them out of their stalls and give them some grass to eat. By the last day though, there was hardly any grass left on that hill. So I know they definitely must have been glad to get back to their own paddocks when we brought them home yesterday.

It's amazing because almost from the minute the three of us were together, Nikita, Jaz and I hit it off almost instantly. Mom said that it's lovely how quickly we all became friends. I guess when you're the same age and you have exactly the same interest – ours of course is our obsession with horses – the rest is easy. Especially when the girls are as nice as Nikita and Jaz.

Out of all the classes, we definitely did enjoy jumping the most. Although, the flatwork classes were really good too. We practiced our rider class skills and really improved our overall riding technique – working on canter leads and learning how to change them smoothly. It felt really good to be learning how to ride so well. And the good part was that we were in a huge undercover arena, out of the hot sun, so that made it even more enjoyable.

In the theory class we focused on all you need to know about caring for a horse and looking after a horse. The instructor brought a horse in to demonstrate. We also had to learn the names of all the parts of a horse as well as the tack. This was to prepare us for a written and practical test on the second last day. All 3 of us managed to pass the test, thank goodness and we now have our D and D Star certificate in horsemanship. Next year we'll be able to go for our C and C Star certificate. I can hardly wait to go again!

It's hard to say what the most fun part of the whole camp was, because I loved it all!!

Even cleaning out the stables was fun! Each morning, we'd have to take turns with the wheelbarrow to clear out all the manure and get fresh sawdust to put down. I've always wanted stables like that at home. And doing this job together with the other girls made me really feel like I was actually in the Saddle Club.

Another fun thing we found to do was to skip with a long rope that we found, during the afternoons when we had some free time. Mom tied one end of it to the main stable entrance door and turned the other end for us while we took turns jumping. This just added to all the fun we had together.

We had a really good camping spot too. And Jaz was also camping there with her Dad, not too far from Jo, Nikita and I. Mom came every day and spent the day there with us then Dad and Nate would come later in the afternoon when we'd all have dinner together. They got to know the other families as well, so they enjoyed themselves too.

Out of all the nights at camp, definitely the last night was the most special. There was a talent show organized for all the camp participants so Nikita, Jaz and I decided to do something together. We ended up choosing Old MacDonald Had a Farm. (I really don't know whose idea that was!!) But we practiced in the morning then throughout the day whenever we had some spare time. Nikita and I were the horses as well as all the other animals and made the animal noises. Jaz was Old MacDonald and she had to sing the words.

The show was held in the really big arena that has grandstands all around the sides for spectators to sit in and watch the events. When we finished, we could hear our families cheering and whistling. On the night, we thought we were really good, so we were absolutely devastated when we didn't get a prize. But when I think about it now, it's actually a bit embarrassing! Although our parents all agreed that we were definitely the most entertaining!!

Later that night, after we'd been to check on the horses, Nikita, Jaz and I came across an empty stall and because it had started to rain, we all decided to camp in there for the night. The stall was perfectly clean and there was that beautiful horsey smell. It was so much fun. But then just as we were about to go to sleep, we heard footsteps coming. We turned off our torches and tried to hide under our sleeping bags in the dark. Then a torch suddenly shone on us and we knew that we'd been found. It was one of the organizers who was also camping there. She said that she had seen lights and came to check. Luckily for us though, she told us we could stay. She said that we weren't supposed to be in there but it was ok as long as we didn't tell anyone else about it. We agreed and thanked her. We were so lucky. Even the girl's parents, who were camping in there with us, said they felt like naughty little school kids. Ha! Ha!

Then on the very last day, there was a gymkhana. We had to be up very early so we could braid all the horses and get them really clean. We had to wear our pony club competition uniforms and our tack had to be spotless as well. It was really hectic trying to get ready in time and I was so glad that Mom and Dad were there to help me. Tracey, who used to own Tara, came to watch as well and she'd made me another new brow band in my pony club colors. She put it on my bridle for me and it looked really pretty. It was so nice of her to come and to bring a new brow band as well. We didn't tell her that someone had accused her of drugging Tara before selling her to us. We knew that she'd be really offended to even hear of something like that being mentioned. And we knew that it wasn't true anyway.

Our first event was rider class and I was feeling really nervous. Tara had started playing up and I didn't know what was wrong with her. Jaz's dad said that he thought she was in season and was being stirred up by all the geldings. Great! What a time for that to happen!

The judge was Keith Lunn – the top rider class judge who we all know. He's the one who judged this event in the last gymkhana and gave me first place. I knew I should be feeling really confident, but Tara was being so naughty. She was putting her ears back and just not cooperating at all. I felt very upset and I really started freaking out inside. Another girl was also having trouble with her horse and started wrenching at the reins and whipping him because he wouldn't behave. I just kept on going though, trying to keep Tara on the right lead and doing what I asked of her. Meanwhile I attempted to stay as calm as possible. Even though, I really felt on the verge of tears.

Nikita ended up getting first place, Jaz came second and I came third. I was so disappointed!

When Keith gave me my green ribbon though, he told me that he was extremely impressed with the calm way I had handled Tara, rather than getting angry with her and being cruel. He also said that all I had to do was change her canter lead because I was on the wrong one. If I had done that, then I would have come first.

I couldn't believe it. I was really jealous and annoyed that the girls had both beaten me. This is the event that's most important to me. I think rider class proves that you're actually a good rider and only the best riders win it. Why did Tara have to be so naughty?

Even though I was upset, I still congratulated Nikita and Jaz. They deserved to win, because they had ridden really well. I know I shouldn't be so competitive, but I can't help it. I always want to do my best and get a top result. I'm even like this at school.

Jaz's dad then helped me with Tara. He's such a

lovely dad and it was so nice of him to do this. He took her to a vacant spot and spent 10 minutes longeing her for me, which really calmed her down. He's been riding since he was a little boy and knows heaps about horses. He said that maybe she'd just picked up on my nerves and excitement this morning. I should have longed her myself I guess, but we'd been so rushed for time.

She was much better behaved after that, which I was really relieved about because we had jumping next. It was an ideal time event where you have to clear as many jumps as possible and also be as close as possible to the ideal finish time. Tara had a brilliant round – she didn't knock one jump, and I knew that my timing was pretty good. I was so happy when the judge handed me the blue ribbon. That made my day and certainly made up for the Rider Class event, that's for sure!

I then went on to win a ribbon in every single event I went in including a new one that I've never done before – Bonfield Bounce - where you have to jump over barrels lying on their sides. And I ended up coming 2nd!

I was really happy!!!

Nikita and Jaz both won lots of ribbons too and we all agree that this week at camp really was the most fun we've ever had!!!

Now we can't wait to go again next year.

But the best thing is that Nikita, Jaz and I are all really close now and we're going to go riding together as much as possible from now on. It's so good that we have another week of school holidays. We'll definitely have to make the most of it.

Thursday 26 September

My life just gets better and better!

I've just come back from a sleep-over at Nikita's house with Jaz. And our horses slept over as well. It was so cool!

Mom took Tara and I to Nikita's yesterday morning. We're so lucky to be able to use Shelley's float. Her parents are happy for us to use it pretty much any time we want - as long as Shelley isn't using it of course. They're such lovely people. I'm really lucky.

Anyway, we unloaded Tara and put her in the paddock with Nikita and Jo's horses. They have the nicest property and have just finished building their new house.

I'm really envious though, because they've built stables as well. Jo said that it's always been her dream to have a horsey property complete with stables and she is so happy with it all. I can certainly see why. There is a beautiful dam for the horses to drink out of and the property is really pretty. It's very private and they have a lovely flat area where they're even building an arena. There's heaps of trails that lead from their place as well, so they have easy access and don't even have to put their horses on a float to go for a trail ride. On top of that, their stables have a tack room where they can keep all the horse feed and all of their tack. And it's right by their house! I'd love to have a property like this, complete with stables, where I didn't have to walk so far to get to my horses. And especially not have to cross over a creek. Nikita is so lucky!!

I really did have such a great time though. Jaz arrived and we unloaded Jasper then all decided to tack up and go for a ride.

Nikita and Jo have set up some jumps down in their arena area and we were all practicing our jumping. Tara is so good now. I just love jumping and really want to do more of it. The girls told me that there's a cross country event at their pony club each year, so next year we're all going to go in that. I've always wanted to do cross country and I'm sure Tara would be awesome at it.

After our ride, we untacked the horses, hosed them down and went in for lunch. Nikita and her family are all vegetarians (except her dad). I haven't tried vegetarian food before but Jo is the best cook. She made us a delicious lunch and dinner as well. Jaz is quite a fussy eater and there's lots of food she doesn't like, but I ate everything and even asked for seconds. Nikita's parents loved it – especially her dad. He said that I'm welcome anytime!

After dinner, we played some board games. I took my Saddle Club board game with me and the girls really enjoyed that. We have so much in common, especially because of the horses. All we care about and talk about is horses. It's so awesome!!

We went riding again today and Nikita and Jo took us on the trails at the back of their house. There are lots of little jumps through there and it was heaps of fun.

I had such a great time and the girls are definitely my best friends now. We've decided to have another horsey sleep-over in 2 weeks' time. It'll either be at my house or at Jaz's. We haven't decided yet.

I love the girls! I'm so glad we're friends!!!

Thursday 3 October

Poor little Soxy has a broken foot! We found him limping around yesterday and realized that he couldn't put pressure on it. So Dad took him to the vet to get him checked out.

They had to x-ray his foot and it turned out that one of his toes is actually broken. He had to stay there overnight and Dad went to collect him this afternoon. His foot and leg are all bandaged up and we have to keep him inside until it heals. He looks so cute with a bandage on his leg but it's going to be a real challenge keeping him in. Luckily the weather is still quite cool as we keep all the doors that lead to our decks closed during winter and the colder months. During summer, we have the house completely open because it gets so hot. So it would be impossible to keep him in then. The risk is that if he tries to climb a tree, he could really injure himself. The vet said that's probably how he did it in the first place. Jumping down from the high part of a tree and landing awkwardly on his foot.

He can still move around on 3 legs and it's the cutest thing to watch him – especially with one leg all bandaged. He's such an affectionate and cuddly cat.

Saturday 5 October

It's been a challenge keeping Soxy in the house. If someone forgets to shut a door leading outside, then sure enough, even if he's sleeping somewhere, he seems to know and off he goes – bandaged leg and all. He's so quick! We've learned that we can't chase him – otherwise he'll take off. But if we just approach him slowly and say – Soxy, Soxy – in a calm quiet voice, he just drops to the ground and rolls over, hoping to be picked up and cuddled.

He's just the cutest!!

I practiced some jumping with Ali, Cammie and Grace in the paddock today and I actually managed to clear 2 and a half feet. That's the highest I've jumped on Tara so far and I feel really proud. My aim is to get to just over 3 feet if I can. Ali jumps that height easily on Bailey. She's thinking about joining a jumping club and I'd love to join that too. I think jumping is my favorite thing to do.

I'm going to talk to Mom about it. Maybe next year, I'll be able to join. That's as long as I can still do pony club as well though.

Sunday 13 October

This weekend was awesome!!!

Nikita and Jaz came to my house for a horsey sleep-over and we had so much fun!

They arrived yesterday morning and we unloaded their horses then put them in the front paddock where we used to agist Cappy. It's perfect having that paddock – we'll always be able to keep their horses there when they come to stay.

We had some lunch and played with Sheba and Soxy for a bit. The girls are the biggest animal lovers and they love my pets. Nikita wants to take Soxy home, she loves him so much. But everyone adores Soxy – and Sheba too of course.

In the afternoon, we all went to tack up so we could go for a ride. We practiced all the sporting events and jumping as well. It's perfect because we're all pretty much the same level when it comes to riding and we all like doing the same things. After our ride, we untacked the horses, gave them a big feed and went back to the house to play some games.

Nikita and Jaz love board games and that's what we did – we played the Saddle Club game of course, because that's our favorite and then we played a heap of other games as well.

After dinner, we just hung out in my bedroom and talked about horses. That's pretty much all we ever talk about when we're together. The 3 of us are definitely horse mad. That's why we get along so well.

We didn't go to sleep until very late – there was too much horsey stuff to talk about. Mom always asks -Why is it called a sleep-over when kids never seem to sleep? I just think there's too much fun to be had to be wasting time sleeping, especially when you've got your best friends staying the night.

Today, we took the horses down the road to the vacant block – just for something different. Mom and Sheba came down with us, to make sure we stayed safe. I think the girls and I would have fun wherever we went, as long as we're together.

Next time, we're going to have a sleep-over at Jaz's house. She's got about 50 acres of land and a lovely arena as well - that will be really cool!

It's absolutely awesome having pony pals for best friends. I'm so lucky!!

Sunday 27 October

Pony Club was heaps of fun today as usual. Except it was so hot. The moms had to bring around cups of water for all the riders and we had to make sure that the horses had plenty of water as well.

There's only two more sessions of pony club left now for this year. But I found out today that for the last session we have a fancy dress day. And not only the riders have to dress up but the horses as well. That will be really fun! I'm going to have to think of something really cool for Tara and I. Apparently some of the girls went to heaps of trouble last year and one girl even painted black stripes on her white pony so he looked like the pony in the movie, Racing Stripes. How cool is that!!! She won first prize but I'm not surprised. Going to all that effort is amazing. Imagine trying to get your horse clean afterwards though. It'd be terrible if the paint didn't come off! I wonder what type of paint she used, anyway.

I have lots to look forward to because my birthday is coming up in only two weeks and my party is the weekend after that. So I'll have to hand out my invitations soon. Of course, I'll invite Nikita and Jade – they're top on my list. And hopefully, Cammie and Grace will come too. I'm not sure about Shelley and Ali – I'll ask

them but they're probably a bit too old to want
to come.

I think I'd better double check my list now, in
case I've left anyone off. So far I have 18 names.
Mom is hoping that some won't be able to come
because we're not sure if they'll all fit in our
music studio. Last year, we camped in tents but
it rained and we got a bit wet. So this year, just
for something different, we're going to sleep on
mattresses on the floor up at Dad's music studio.
At least we'll be away from the house and can
make as much noise as we want.

I can't wait!!!!!!

Sunday 3 November

I'm so excited thinking about my birthday. There's only 8 days to go now and then another 5 days until my party. Everyone at school is really looking forward to it. A lot of the same friends came last year and they had so much fun, they can't wait to come again.

They love coming to my house, especially because I have a horse. But now I have a new horse to show them and I still have Sparkle as well. We're going to set up a disco in our gazebo again too. I can't wait!

Monday 11 November

Today is my birthday and I had such a great day!

Mom made me a cake to take to school. Some kids don't bring cakes on their birthdays but I always do. Mrs Johnson even asked for the recipe. I didn't tell her that Mom made it from a packet mix though! Mom said she was glad about that. □

As soon as Mom came home from work this afternoon, I opened my presents. I always do this because it would be such a rush in the morning and this way, I have something to really look forward to all day!

I got so much lovely horsey stuff - a brand new black, velvet competition helmet (I've been borrowing an old one up until now) and also a beautiful bright pink cover that I can use to put over the top of it when I'm not riding in competitions. These covers look so cool and are great to keep helmets protected and still looking perfect. It's almost like having 2 different helmets as well. Mom said at least I'll stand out when I'm wearing it. She'll just have to look out for the bright pink head bobbing up and down at pony club.

As well, Mom and Dad also gave me some brand new riding boots that I can keep especially for pony club and competitions. From now on, I'll just wear my old ones in the paddock. And I got a lovely white saddle cloth that'll look so pretty on Tara's chestnut coat.

Out of everything, I really love the Giddy Up Girl t-shirts that Mom bought for me. It's a new brand of riding gear for girls and the clothes are so cool. They come in heaps of pretty colors and have lots of different sayings on them. One of my t-shirts says – Funky Filly – and the other one says – Ride for Your Life. I also got some Giddy Up Girl PJs that have horses all over them.

I'll be able to wear those at my slumber party on Saturday.

I'm really looking forward to it!

I'm so lucky - 2 cakes in one day!!

Sunday 17 November

I had the best party! But I'm really sad that it's over. I wish it was Saturday morning and I could have it all over again!!!

When everyone arrived, we went straight up to the music studio and set up our mattresses and sleeping gear. It was pretty cramped and a couple of girls had to share a mattress but we all managed to fit.

Cammie and Grace remembered a lot of people from my party last year, but I had to introduce Nikita and Jaz because they didn't know anyone. That was ok though, because everyone made them feel really welcome and I could see that they were already fitting in and having a great time.

Before we did anything, everyone wanted to see Tara. All my school friends have heard so much about her from me and also from Tina. Tina's been over lots of times and she's told everyone at school about how beautiful Tara is. I gave everyone some cut up carrots and a handful of hay, so they could feed both Tara and Sparkle. Of course when the horses saw the food, they both came trotting over. Because there were so many of us, I made everyone stay in the small paddock and pat the horses over the fence. I certainly didn't want to risk any accidents.

Everyone loved my babies – I knew they would!

Then we all got our togs on and hopped into the pool. Dad set up all his musical equipment again. So we turned the music up really loud. What's a party without loud music anyway?

All my friends just love our diving deck – it really is the best thing ever. And their favorite thing to do is line-up, hold hands and run and jump in together. The trampoline is awesome fun as well and lots of us were jumping off the tramp and into the pool. Mom was a bit worried about this but we were all having so much fun, she just stayed close and kept an eye on us.

This year, rather than giving everyone pony rides, which takes so much time and quite a bit of effort, Nate gave everyone a motor bike ride. Some of the girls were too scared but most of them had a ride and they loved it.

That's what is so awesome about our place – there's so many different things to do!

I even made a horsey piñata for us. I made Tara in paper mache and everyone thought it was so cool!

After dinner, we had a disco in the gazebo. We played all the fun games like the limbo, freeze and musical chairs. Mom bought heaps of prizes, so that made the games really fun. And the girls absolutely loved the prizes that they got. I went shopping with Mom earlier this week and picked out a special little gift for each of my friends. I had little fun prizes for each of them and also something special - mainly jewelry or things for their hair. I made sure everyone got something that they would really like and it was great fun because I could see that they really loved them.

I was so pleased!

Then we all went off in pairs or small groups to put something together for a talent show. Nate was the judge and I could tell that he really enjoyed having that job – I guess it made him feel important in front of my friends. I actually think he secretly likes a couple of them as well.

Nikita, Jade and I decided to do our Old MacDonald act from pony club camp. But we were laughing so much, we could barely sing. It turned into a comedy and at least everyone had a laugh.

Nate chose 3 of my friends who sang a song together, as the winners – (these are the ones he likes, so no wonder he chose them).

After that, everyone had turns at singing into the microphone. Of course Tina hogged it again. She can't help herself. I really think she would love to be a rock star. But I had a go too. It is kind of addictive and I think that a lot of people would secretly love to perform on stage.

When it got to around 11pm, Mom and Dad thought that the neighbors needed to get some sleep, so they made us turn the music off and head up to the studio.

It took a while for everyone to get changed into their PJs, clean their teeth and use the bathroom. It was pitch black by then and there's no light to show us the way. So we all had torches and went together. The girls who live in the suburbs are all such scaredy cats – they were screaming and saying they'd seen a snake or a strange animal or whatever. Talk about drama queens!

Anyway, we didn't get much sleep, that's for sure. Mom and Dad were so glad that we were away from the house because they didn't hear a thing!

This morning, we just woke up and had breakfast, then swam in the pool until everyone was picked up around lunch time. Tina was back on the microphone though, the first chance she got.

I knew she would be!

It really was the best party. I think each year my parties just get better and better!!!

Sunday 24 November

I just couldn't decide what to go as to the pony club fancy dress day. I wish Nikita and Jade went to my pony club. It would have been heaps of fun planning our costumes and all going together.

In the end, I decided on being a pirate. Dad took me to the 2nd hand shop and I was able to get all the things I needed for Tara and myself. I put a scarf on Tara and painted a black circle around her eye but didn't do too much else. I had to be careful, as I didn't want to put anything on that would frighten her – she's such a chicken!

Everyone arrived in fancy dress and some of the girls put in heaps of effort! They must have been up before sunrise to get their horses ready! There was a Santa Claus, a couple of ballerinas with horses in tutus which looked so cute, a girl dressed as Zorro and another pirate like me – her costume was probably a bit better than mine. She actually really did look like Johnny Depp from Pirates of the Caribbean. She wore a beard and a long black wig. She'd also painted white skulls and crossbones on her horse. I thought that was very clever.

They gave out prizes for first, second and third place. The other pirate got 3rd. I didn't win a prize but that's ok because the day was still great fun!

We did all the usual classes that we normally do except in the afternoon, we played polo. It's actually quite tricky trying to hit that ball while you're riding, especially if you have a bit of speed up.

I'm just sad now to think that pony club is over and I have to wait about 2 months for it to start again. At least we still have presentation night to go which will be exciting.

Maybe I'll be able to convince Nikita and Jade to come to my pony club next year.

That really would be awesome!

Sunday 8 December

Last night, we had pony club presentation night and I loved it!

All the families came and we had a barbecue dinner before the awards were presented. The kids were all running around in the arena and playing chasing games. One of the other girls has a brother Nate's age and they got on really well. It was good to see that Nate enjoyed himself and wasn't complaining about being bored, because he originally hadn't been keen to go.

The coolest thing was that they hired a mechanical bull and all the kids got to line up and have turns. I lasted for quite a while before I was bucked off! I'm just glad they had padded mattresses on the floor around it, so it didn't really hurt when you fell.

All the pony club members were given a medallion and a maroon cap with our pony club logo on it. Then the major awards were given out. Everyone has accumulated points throughout the year from all the gymkhanas, shows and events that they've competed in and these points had to be handed into the pony club secretary so she could tally them up. I haven't been to many events because Sparkle got sick and Tara had a sore back for a while. So I missed out on a few of the gymkhanas that I would've liked to have gone to.

But that's ok – next year I plan to go to every gymkhana that's being held. And I'm sure I'll do really, really well.

I did get 4th place for best presented though which was such a nice surprise. I always try my hardest to have Tara looking her best for pony club each week and spend lots of time cleaning my tack. The Stuben takes quite a while to clean as well, but obviously it was worth the effort. And it's so good to be able to still get a prize even though I have an old saddle.

It was a really fun night and I'm looking forward to next year already!

At least we only have two more weeks of school left before the Xmas holidays. Then 6 weeks off! Yayyyyyyyyyyy!!!!

Nikita, Jade and I wanted to have lots of horsey sleep-overs but they'll both be away for most of the holidays. I was so disappointed when they told me! At least I'll still be able to ride with Shelley, Ali, Cammie and Grace. None of them are going away anywhere, so thank goodness I'll have them to ride with.

I'm looking forward to doing lots of riding in the holidays and improving my jumping even more.

It'd be great to be able to surprise everyone at pony club next year.

That would be really cool!

I can't wait to try the mechanical bull again! ☺

Friday 13 December

The worst thing happened this afternoon and I feel sick thinking about it.

It all started because my parents had an argument with Cammie and Grace's dad, Jim. Now he's taken their horses out of our paddocks where he was keeping them and has moved them over to Ali's next door.

Normally on a Friday afternoon, Shelley comes over and we go riding with the other girls in our two paddocks. They're the best places for us to ride because there's a lovely flat area almost like an arena in the small paddock. We also have all the jumps and the sporting equipment set up in the larger paddock. And as well as that, we have a lovely hill that is perfect to trot up and down on so we can build up the horses' muscle tone.

Anyway, Shelley arrived and fetched Millie so she could take her up to the shed and tack her up. This was unusual as we normally take our saddles and bridles over to the horses and tack up in the paddock, rather than make two trips.

After waiting for a while at the house for Shelley and Millie to come down, I realised that they had actually disappeared. Mom and I couldn't work out where they'd gone. So we decided to head on over to the paddock, thinking that they might already be there.

It was when we crossed the creek, that we got the shock of our lives!

Ali, Cammie and Grace were all on their horses but on the other side of the fence. And riding with them, in Ali's paddock, was Shelley. I could see them all staring at me. I waved but they didn't wave back.

That was when I started to feel sick in the stomach.

I instantly knew it was because of the argument with Jim. I also knew that it meant the girls weren't going to ride with me anymore.

And there I was in our huge paddock on Tara, riding around, all on my own.

Mom kept telling me not to worry, to just ignore them and keep riding. But I knew that she was just as upset as me.

I kept glancing over in their direction – I just couldn't help it. Especially because all I could hear was their laughter and constant chatter. There they were, doing what all horse mad girls do together when they're riding – laughing, chatting and having heaps of fun.

Shelley is really good friends with Ali – they're similar ages and they're even at the same school together now, whereas, I'm much younger. So I guess I can understand why she'd rather ride with her.

But meanwhile I was left - miserable - on Tara - in our huge paddock - on my own. It took all the effort I had not to burst into tears.

I had originally thought it would be so much fun having our very own saddle club. But Mom says that when you get a group of girls together, over a period of time, problems are often sure to break out. It's the same at school with some of the girls in my class who are lways arguing.

And then on top of the competitive and possessive personalities in our horsey group, actually adding real live horses to the mix as well as interfering and over-protective parents, can make everything fall apart. Which is exactly what's happened!!

But what am I supposed to do now???

It's almost the Christmas holidays.

Am I supposed to ride on my own every day while they're on the other side of the fence having all the fun – right where I can not only hear them but also constantly see them??

I know I have Nikita and Jaz to ride with now and I am so grateful for that. But they're going away for pretty much the whole 6 weeks of the holidays and even when they're here, we can only ride together occasionally. It's not the same as having someone right next door to ride with. Nikita has her mom and Jaz has her sister and her dad to ride with anytime they want. But who do I have??

Nobody!!!

Just thinking about this afternoon and watching them over there together, makes me feel not only sick in the stomach, but really sad!

IT'S NOT FAIR!!!

I feel so upset just thinking about it.

I think I'd rather not ride at all!

Maybe that's what I should do!

It's all too hard. Maybe I should just stop riding once and for all!

But the question is…Can I really give it all up???

***

Book 5

Dream Pony Disasters

Friday 3 January

MOM!! DAD!!! HURRRRY - TARA'S HURT!!!!! I
was hysterical with fear that my baby was going
to die. I tried desperately to help her, but there
was nothing I could do.

The words I kept screaming this afternoon and
the vision of my baby, in the paddock, covered
in blood, is one I'll never forget. And I cannot
get that nightmare out of my head.

I've hardly ridden in weeks! I haven't wanted to.
So often I've heard the girl's voices over at Ali's
– laughing, giggling, chatting and having fun.
Shelley keeps telling me that I should just go
over and ride with them. But how can I when
I'm not welcome?

I've had small rides on Tara, on my own of
course. And I've seen the girls occasionally, but
it's like I'm not even there. They just tack up and
head off down the driveway. I guess they're
riding on the property at the end of our street.
Shelley said that they've met the lady who lives
down there and she's invited them to ride in her
arena. She doesn't have horses anymore and
said it never gets used. Can you believe that? A
proper arena as well as really nice trails that are
available to use any time and they're just down
the road! Available for them, that is. Shelley says
it's great – but I don't want to know about it

because I'm stuck here on my own!

Anyway, Shelley called during the week to tell us that she's moving Millie to a new property because it's much closer to her house. I was so upset to hear that they were going. I don't get to ride with Shelley much but she's like my big sister and Tara and Sparkle are really attached to Millie as well. Then on top of that, Dad found a new home for Sparkle! I couldn't believe it when he told me. She's going to a family with two little girls – they just want an older pony for their girls to be led around on. I know that Sparkle will be perfect for that and she'll get the attention she deserves. I admit that I've been neglecting her but I still wanted to be able to keep her. She was my very first pony – the pony I learned to ride on. And selling her has led to a near disaster!

Today was the day it all happened. Shelley came to collect Millie this morning. And that was really sad. Then Sparkle's new owners arrived this afternoon. It was too much to take in - all in one day. They seem nice and it's good that she'll be with people who will care for her, but I was incredibly upset to see her go. I have tears in my eyes right now just thinking about her.

After Sparkle left, I decided to go and check on Tara and it's so lucky that I did – although I certainly was not prepared for what I found!

Tara was completely tangled up in a section of barbed wire fencing. And the more she tried to escape, the more tangled she became. She was so distressed – it was terrible. She must have totally freaked out when we took Sparkle out of the paddock and across the creek. Sparkle is her best friend and I think Tara knew that she was being taken somewhere, then she became totally distressed about it! She must have tried to chase after Sparkle and rammed into the fence. The barbed wire had been put in the paddock by the original owners of our property when they had cattle years ago. We always knew that it wasn't suitable for horses, but it hasn't been a problem until now.

Oh my gosh, it was such a shock to see her trapped like that! I just kept screaming out – MOM!! DAD!!! HURRRRY - TARA'S HURT!!!!! I couldn't leave her. The more she tried to move, the more tangled she became and I could see she had cuts everywhere!

Thank goodness Mom and Dad heard me screaming and came racing over, totally unprepared of course for the mess that Tara was suddenly in. What a nightmare! The memory of her being tangled up like that today, makes me feel sick.

Dad had to get some wire cutters while I tried to keep her calm. This was one of the hardest things for me to do, because I was freaking out myself. Luckily, the vet arrived quickly and was able to give her a needle to calm her down. He also gave her a huge shot of antibiotics as well as an injection for tetanus. After cleaning her wounds, we found that it looked much worse than it actually really was – there had been blood everywhere so we'd thought that it was extremely bad. But thankfully, the vet said that the antibiotics should do the trick. Although we're now going to have to inject her ourselves, every day for the next week. I'm glad that Dad has agreed to take that job on. I think he feels guilty about Sparkle going. If she were still in the paddock, this would never have happened. The vet is coming back tomorrow to check on Tara. My poor baby! How is she going to cope now that her paddock mate has gone? They were so close. And how am I going to cope? There's photos of me and Sparkle all around my room. The new owners said we can visit her, but it's not the same. I already miss her so much.

I can't believe that I was actually thinking about giving up riding! Now that Sparkle's gone and I came close to losing Tara, it makes me realize how much I love horses – especially my beautiful girl. She's my dream pony and as soon as she gets better, I'm riding. Every day!! How could I have wanted to stop my most favorite thing in the whole world - all because of a friendship problem with my neighbors?

Well it's not going to stop me anymore. Nikita and Jaz will be back from their holidays soon anyway, so I can ride with them. And even when they're not around, I'll just ride on my own.

My poor baby! I hope she recovers soon!!

I love riding so much!

How could I ever give up???

Saturday 4 January

Poor Tara – there's cuts all over her legs and front. Most of them are pretty minor though, which is so lucky and hopefully they won't scar. I bathed all her wounds again today and Dad gave her the antibiotic injection. She stayed so calm the whole time – she's such a beautiful pony! I just hope she doesn't get depressed about Sparkle going. Luckily she can see Ali's horses over the fence. I found her there today just staring into the other paddock, watching them graze. I feel so sorry for her!

Dad said that maybe we can try to get someone else to agist their horse here. That way, she'll have company and it won't cost us any money. Sparkle was costing us quite a lot with all her special feed and arthritis supplements. I hope her new owners keep them up – they said they will – so hopefully they do.

The vet said that as long as all goes well, I should be able to ride Tara within the next 2 weeks. And that's perfect timing, because Nikita will be back by then. Jaz will also be back soon after, so we'll all be able to ride together.

I feel so happy just thinking about the 3 of us riding together again. And thank goodness my baby is going to be ok!!

Wednesday 15 January

Tara is doing really well. I spent time longeing her this morning and she seemed absolutely fine. I had been very worried that she'd be permanently lame, but her wounds have healed beautifully. Once the hair grows back, there should be no scarring at all, which is great. She's such a pretty pony and it would be a shame to have a heap of scars across her legs and front.

I'm really looking forward to doing lots of gymkhanas this year. I think I'll try cross country as well. Nikita and Jaz have told me all about the cross country event that's held at their pony club and I think Tara will be great at this.

I can't wait for pony club to start again in a few weeks. I wonder if I can convince Nikita and Jaz to change clubs and join mine – it really is the best one after all!

Saturday 18 January

Ali's mom rang today and convinced my mom to go over and make amends with our neighbor, Jim. Mom had decided that enough was enough. She's been so upset about the whole argument they had and hates seeing me miserable. So that's what we did. Mom and I went over to Ali's and walked down the road to the arena with all the other girls and their parents. Mom and Jim had a big chat and sorted everything out. And the girls were really nice to me. They said that they've missed me and were very worried about Tara after her accident. I had the best time with them today – and that arena is so cool. There's even jumps and sporting equipment for us to use as well. And the best news is that Tara was perfect! I had a wonderful ride on her and I think that she enjoyed it as much as me!

Mom told me tonight that we both have to learn from the drama with our neighbors – communication is definitely the way to sort out problems and if there's a problem, you just need to talk about it! I'm going to remember that at school from now on or anytime I have a problem with friends. By talking problems through, they can often be easily resolved- rather than letting a small issue become something huge.

That's a really good lesson, I think!

Monday 20 January

Nikita's back! And she came over with her new pony, Latte today. It's great to have her here – I've missed her so much. And Latte is really pretty!! He's a 14 hand paint and his name suits him perfectly. Her last horse Darcy slipped and fell in the paddock and really injured his back. So he's gone to a new property that is flat and much more suitable for him in his condition. Darcy's such a cute, cheeky pony. Hopefully, he'll get better soon!

But Nikita and I had the best time together today! We went down the road to the arena and it was heaps of fun. It's so exciting to be riding in a real arena! It's great to do something different and Nikita and Latte really enjoyed it as well. We rode on the trails and then did some jumping. I actually jumped over 3 feet. That's the highest I've ever jumped! And Latte is a great jumper too. Mom kept raising the jumps for us because we just kept clearing them. It was so exciting and fun to be jumping really well! And we could tell that the horses were loving it! Nikita is really lucky to have found Latte – he's so beautiful and has the nicest nature! We're now both really excited to do the cross country event that's coming up soon and also to compete in the next gymkhana – especially the jumping.I think this year, we're all going to do really well!

Saturday 1 February

Unbelievable! I don't know how else to describe what happened today!!! I feel really sick just thinking about it...

A friend of Dad's came over with her 2 children. Her husband recently died of cancer which is very sad, and he was one of Dad's best friends. So Dad was keen to make sure they had some fun while they were at our house.

Everything was going well until Kelly, the 10 year old daughter hopped on Tara to have a ride. Mom was leading her around the paddock and when she said that she could ride, Mom unhooked the lead rope and walked along beside her. Tara was walking calmly around but Kelly decided that was too boring. She started to kick Tara really hard and call out – Yah! Yah! Yah! Tara went into a small trot but Kelly kept kicking her and calling out. Mom then went to grab the reins but it was too late!

Tara had decided to bolt!

And Kelly began to scream!!

And she just kept on screaming!!!

This frightened Tara so much that she went into a canter and then suddenly she was in a full gallop. She was racing around and around our smaller paddock – which is probably about 300 feet long. I quickly ran to shut the gate because if she had decided to go into the big paddock, I dread to think what could have happened!

Every time Tara galloped past us, we tried to grab her reins but couldn't get hold of them. She was going way too fast and we could not stop her.

It was one of the scariest things I've ever seen! There was this young girl, absolutely freaking out, on a runaway horse – my horse – in my paddock – and there was nothing we could do. The more Kelly screamed, the more frightened Tara became and she just continued galloping at full speed. I kept on thinking – please, please stop screaming!

Everyone was freaking out! Me, Mom, Dad and of course, Kelly's little brother and her mom. Dad said later, all he could think about was that Kelly's mom had just lost her husband to cancer and there was a huge chance she was going to lose her daughter as well.

It was absolutely terrifying!!!!!!!!

We kept yelling at Kelly to pull on the reins, but she couldn't hear us. The sound of her screams and Tara's hooves as they thundered past was deafening! Eventually, she decided of her own accord, that when Tara slowed down at a corner, she would just fall off. And that was exactly what she did! She was so brave to do that! But we couldn't believe that she wasn't hurt – except for the mental trauma of what she had just been through! She was badly shaken and crying but there were no cuts or injuries at all.

When we talked about it later, visions of terrible things kept coming to us – Kelly could have fallen off and been badly injured or thrown onto the barbed wire fence and scarred for life! She could have ended up in a wheelchair or she could have been trampled and killed!!

I don't know if Kelly will ever ride a horse again. So much for entertaining them. They won't forget their visit to our place, that's for sure. And neither will we! My heart is racing now, just thinking about it!! It's a memory I'd really rather forget!

Sunday 16 February

Pony club started again today. It was so good to be back there and great to see all the girls. Tara behaved perfectly as well. Her cuts are completely healed and she looked beautiful. I actually got 10 out of 10 for line up this morning. It was such a great way to start the day.

I'd been a bit worried about her after the incident with Kelly. She really was a psycho horse that day but I know it was because Kelly frightened her so much. And Tara does get spooked fairly easily. Ever since though, she's been fine which is such a relief. I definitely didn't want to have to go through more dramas with her behavior.

And the cross country event at Nikita and Jaz's pony club is next weekend. I'm really excited about that. It should be great fun!

Sunday 23 February

Today was amazing! I absolutely love cross country!

To begin with, Tara was quite stirred up. I don't know if it was from all the excitement and people everywhere or whether she picked up on my nerves. Thank goodness, Jaz's dad came to the rescue again and helped with longeing her in a vacant paddock. This made a huge difference.

Before starting, we were able to do some practice cross country jumps, in our age groups. Everything was going really well, but then as I headed Tara towards the last jump, I lost my balance and fell off. That really shook me up. It's pretty scary when you fall off. Mom and Dad came running over, but I was okay. I hadn't hurt myself at all. But it wasn't good for my confidence, I know that much.

I still felt a little shaken when it was our turn to begin the event. Everyone had to go one after the other. It's the best cross country track – there are so many different kinds of jumps –logs and fallen down trees, man-made jumps and even stretches of water. Tara wasn't sure about those and I had to walk her across a couple of narrow creeks, but that was fine. It was really exciting and heaps of fun. There was even a professional photographer there and we managed to buy a fantastic photo of me jumping Tara. I'm so glad to have it – she looks absolutely gorgeous. I've glued my photo onto the front of my diary.

It was a pretty eventful day and although I was quite nervous, it was still really exciting to be doing something so different. I also met all the girls who go to that pony club and they were really friendly. Nikita and Jaz are desperately trying to convince me to change from my pony club, and I must admit, I'm actually pretty tempted. It would be so nice to go to pony club with my best horsey friends. That would make it heaps more fun. Mom said that I need to think about it first and not rush into it, so that's what I'll do. If I do move though, it definitely won't be until after our club gymkhana which is coming up in a few weeks' time. It's the first gymkhana for the season and I can't wait!

Sunday 2 March

Jaz and I have been at Nikita's all weekend for a horsey sleep-over. And today, we decided to make some horsey muffins. I always get really annoyed because we never seem to have the ingredients at my house, so I can never make them. Whereas Nikita always has a supply that she has made! At least I get to make them when I go to her house, I guess. Anyway, they turned out really well and the horses absolutely loved them!

We've now decided to make a book of recipes, get some copies printed and sell them at our pony clubs. I think they'll be really popular. For our gymkhana, I'm going to make a batch of horsey treats and sell them there as well. All the members have to take a plate of home-made snacks to sell as this raises money for the club. But no-one ever thinks of the horses. My treats will probably be snapped up!

Wednesday 5 March

Today I tried something really different. Mom has been trying to convince me to play netball but I haven't been the least bit interested. She used to play it when she was young and said that she thought I'd enjoy it too. She says that team sports are a great thing for kids to be involved in and very different to horse riding, where even though you can ride with friends, you're not part of a team.

Anyway, when Dad picked me up from school this afternoon, he persuaded me to go down to the netball courts where the team was training. Then before I knew it, the coach had put a team shirt on me and I was on the court.

I've watched Nate play basketball before but netball is very different to that and it took me a while to get used to the rules. At least in netball we don't have to bounce the ball, we just have to throw it to each other. But then once we have the ball, we can't run, we have to pass it to someone else. The other tricky thing is that there's no backboard when shooting goals into the hoop. I've watched Nate bounce the basketball off the backboard which makes it much easier to score than in netball. So, it's quite different in lots of ways. But netball is so much fun and I can't believe how much I enjoyed it. The girls are really nice and one of my close friends from school plays on the team so that made it even more special.

The look of surprise on Mom's face when I came home this afternoon wearing a netball uniform was hilarious. She certainly hadn't been expecting that, but she is really pleased.

And it shouldn't affect my riding time because netball training is only once a week with games on Saturday mornings. So I can still ride on Saturday afternoons and other weekday afternoons as well.

Our first game is this week and I feel nervous already!

I'm sure Tara won't mind me playing netball

on Saturday mornings! ☺

Sunday 9 March

Pony club was great today but I can't help thinking about how much more fun it would be if I were with Nikita and Jaz. There really aren't any girls my age at my club, they're either younger or older and I don't have any best friends there. I'll have to make a decision soon, I guess.

But today, we were all practicing the sporting events to get ready for the gymkhana in 2 weeks. We had a big meeting as well – there's so much that the members have to do to prepare for it. No wonder each pony club only has one gymkhana per year!

And yesterday, I had my first official netball game. I'm playing defence, because I'm quite tall and I'm actually pretty good at it. The best news is though, that we won our first game for the season. It was so cool!!

For the next 2 weeks, on the afternoons that I don't have netball, I'm going to have to work hard with Tara and try to get some last minute training in before the gymkhana. I really hope that I do well. Nikita is competing in it too but she's in a different age group. I'm glad I don't have to compete against her because that would be tough. She's been jumping so well on Latte and he's very quick as well – so he'd be hard to beat.

I really want to do better in this gymkhana than I have in any other. I guess it's because it's my own club gymkhana and I'd like everyone to see how much my riding has improved. Anyway, regardless of how well I do, I know it's going to be heaps of fun. I can't wait!!

Tonight I found a photo of some beautiful ribbons. I just love gymkhanas...

Sunday 23 March

Today was awesome!!! It was the most exciting gymkhana I've ever been in. I actually won a place in every single event and there were even 14 girls in my group, so I did really well! The best part I think, was winning the jumping. I was so excited to win that. It was an ideal time event. Tara cleared every jump and we were the closest horse and rider to the ideal time. I felt so happy when I was given the blue ribbon. We were also first in bounce pony and even bending as well. I just love those blue ribbons!! But before the bending event, I desperately needed to go to the bathroom. I knew that I didn't have enough time though. So I decided to just stay and do the event because I certainly didn't want to miss it. When I won, Mom said that the smile on my face went from ear to ear!! I think I might have to try that bathroom trick next time – I'm sure it actually made me go faster – which is so funny, don't you think?

Throughout the day, I'd been keeping a tally of my points and I was really hoping that I might have a chance to be the highest point scorer for my group. I've won 3rd and 4th place before and got a trophy for each which was great, but that's the best I've ever done.

Of course I was absolutely over the moon when my name was announced at the presentation for being first in my age group – I was so happy! And that first place trophy is much bigger than any of the others that I've ever won. It looks really impressive.

After that, we were just about to head home when the president of our pony club told Mom that we should stay a bit longer, although we had no idea why. We had to wait until all the age groups had been presented and then all of a sudden, these two huge trophies appeared. I felt like I was dreaming when my name was called out as winner of the perpetual trophy for highest point scorer from our entire pony club in the 12 years and under age group. And I thought that the first place trophy was impressive! These ones are huge!!

I think this is one of the most exciting things that's ever happened to me – apart from getting my two beautiful horses of course!

What a day! I have the biggest smile on my face right now! And as well as that, all my horsey treats sold really quickly. Some people were even asking me for the recipe. I told them that our recipe book will be available soon. I think it'll be a best seller!

Thursday 27 March

We have a new paddock mate for Tara! I'm so happy and I'm sure Tara will be as well.

Dad put a sign on the noticeboard at the stock feeds store and a girl called Tammy responded to the ad. She called last night and has two horses. One of them is a little Shetland pony named Bonnie. Tammy is 17, she doesn't do pony club or compete at all but she's always had horses from a young age. Because of the serious drought we've been having, she has very little grass left in her paddock so she needs somewhere to keep her horses until next summer.

We're very lucky at our place. Because we have 10 acres and only one horse, we have plenty of grass. So now, Tammy's coming over for a look on Saturday and if she's happy – which I'm sure she will be - she'll bring the horses on Sunday. I can't wait to meet Bonnie. Shetlands are so cute!

Yayy!! Now we have new friends for Tara.

Oh my gosh, I hope they get on well!

Sunday 30 March

Tammy's horses arrived today and Tara was very curious to find out who the new girls were. As soon as she saw them, her ears went forward and she came trotting over. She's such a sweetie!

I'm glad they're not geldings – that would probably cause big problems, with Tara going into season all the time. But anyway, they both seem nice and quiet and were very happy to graze on the grass in their new paddock. We've given them the small paddock next to Tara, until they get used to each other.

I think this should work out well!

And that Shetland is adorable!

Bonnie is really cute!

Saturday 5 April

Today after our club netball game, which we won – AGAIN – I decided to try out for the local representative team. I know I haven't been playing for very long but Alex, my coach, convinced me to give it a go. She thinks that I'm a natural netballer and that I'm playing really well. I have heaps of lovely friends who also tried out and if we all get in, it would be so much fun! The uniforms are really cool too – pink shirts with a black pleated skirt and we even get to go away on carnivals for a whole weekend at a time.

I think I actually played very well in the trials, but we won't find out till next week, if we have made the team. The coach has said that she'll call us. I feel nervous just thinking about it.

Right now, I'm going to make a sign and put it on my bedroom wall…I am now in the representative netball team and I am so excited!!

Mom brought an awesome book home for me to read recently and it's all about creating what you want in life. It's such an incredible book, I just loved it! The story is about a girl around my age who goes to a new school and shows her friends how to set goals and achieve them. It's a great story as well and I really got into it. As well as that, I've actually learned so much from it! One of the main points is that you should set your goals, write them down and then focus on them every day. Then you'll have a better chance of making them happen. You also need to visualize in your mind, what you want to achieve. The girl in the story says…If you see it, you can believe it. And if you believe it, you can achieve it!

So I'm going to do that every day and every night from now on!!

I made a sign and I'm going to put it on my wall where I can look at it each day. It says…

"I AM NOW ON THE REPRESENTATIVE NETBALL TEAM AND I AM SO EXCITED!!!"

Sunday 6 April

Another day of drama! Why do these things always happen to us?

Today, Mom and I set out early with Tara in the trailer. I'm really lucky because even though Shelley has moved Millie to another property, they've decided to keep their horse float at our house so we can pretty much use it whenever we want. This is the luckiest thing – otherwise I'd be stranded and wouldn't be able to go anywhere.

We were on our way to a CTR event – (CTR is short for Competitive Trail Ride). Nikita's mom, Jo is really keen on these and the girls and I decided to give one a try. So Mom and I were all prepared and after making sure that the trailer was securely attached to the tow bar and everything was as it should be, we set off.

I was really excited to be going somewhere completely different and doing something new, especially with my best friends. And today, Jaz and I had planned to compete together as a team. You can also enter the event individually, but we thought that being together would be more fun. Nikita and her mom were riding as a team as well.

So, we drove to the end of the street where we had arranged to wait for Jaz and her dad as the plan was to follow them. We sat there waiting -

we were actually early for once - then before long, we saw them heading towards us.

I waved to Jaz as they drove past and Mom turned on the ignition so that we could drive onto the main road after them. But to our absolute horror, the car wouldn't start! Mom kept trying and trying the ignition but it was no use. That was when I started to panic!

There we were stuck at the edge of the main road, with a horse in a trailer attached to our car and no way of going anywhere. Then out of the blue, the car suddenly started. Mom and I were so happy! We quickly took off but only made it to our local township before the car decided to die again.

We didn't know what we were going to do! Dad wasn't at home and there really wasn't much he could do anyway. Then when Mom tried ringing Jaz's dad, there was no answer! We couldn't believe it! Why weren't they answering and how were we going to let them know what had happened to us?

Luckily, we were able to get in contact with the road service company, although it took quite a while for them to come. In the meantime, I had to hop in the trailer with Tara to try and keep her calm because there was nowhere safe to unload her. The car service man eventually managed to get the engine started again but then told us that we'd be able to get home and no further! At that point I felt like bursting into tears!! He said the car needed repairs and there was no way we could drive any long distances in it, especially towing a horse trailer.

So we had to go home!

I was really disappointed! I knew that Jaz would be too. We were supposed to be riding together. But just as we pulled up at our house and unloaded Tara, a car suddenly pulled up in our driveway. To our absolute amazement, we saw that it was Jaz's dad towing an empty horse float. He had got the text message that mom had sent him and come back to get us!

How nice is that. I am so grateful to him for doing that. I'm definitely going to make him a thank you card and Mom said that we can buy him a present as well. He certainly deserves it!

So, then we had to get Tara back in the float and race to the CTR. Jaz was over the moon to see us and thank goodness, each rider or riding team leaves at different intervals, one after the other, so we weren't too late to start.

All the riders had to follow pink ribbons that were tied to bushes in various places along the trail and there were regular checkpoints that we had to pass through. At each checkpoint, the horses had to pass a test such as having to back up over a log within a certain amount of time or the rider having to carry a plastic bag while riding from one spot to another. And I couldn't believe it, because at the very first checkpoint, Tara got spooked and I could not get her through. She simply would not walk along the length of plastic tarp that was laying on the ground – even though we've practiced doing that at home. In the end, I decided it was no use and just had to go around that one, so obviously we didn't score very well at that particular checkpoint.

Then a bit further down the trail, there was a fork in the track and we weren't sure which way to go. By this time, we were in the middle of the bush somewhere, and we couldn't see any other riders. We decided to take the track on the left and started cantering to make up for lost time. We went a fair way along but there were still no pink ribbons to be seen anywhere! Jaz had been given her mom's phone and tried calling her dad but there was no reception. For the second time in one day, I really started to panic! We were lost in the bush and didn't know which way to go!

All I know now is that today was such an adventure. I don't think we'll ever forget it! Luckily for us, we happened to come across a farm house and Jaz knocked on the door while I held the horses. The lady who lived there was so lovely and thank goodness for that. We were a bit scared about going to a strange person's house in the middle of the bush, but we didn't know what else to do.

She rang Jaz's dad from her home phone and explained where we were. He raced over to the organizers to get help for us and they had to send a rider out to find us and show us the way back.

So obviously, we didn't get a place today – we probably came last because we took so long to complete the course and missed several checkpoints as well. But at least we did manage to eventually get back! Jaz's dad was so relieved to see us. And what a relief it was to see him!

Now that I'm home and the day is over, I find it hard to believe that so many things went wrong today. It's definitely a day I won't forget but one thing is for sure – I don't think I'll go on another CTR in a hurry!*I think I'll leave CTRs to the experts!*

Wednesday 9 April

I could not go to school today. Luckily Mom has Wednesdays off, because there was no way that I could have gone to school!!!

The phone rang this morning and I happened to answer it, which is unusual because I'm always running late and never have time for things like that. Anyway, when I realized it was the representative netball coach actually calling to talk to me, I was so excited. But then, within a split second, my stomach dropped. She said that I played really well at the trials but I didn't make the team. I couldn't believe it!! I passed her onto Mom to speak to, ran into my room and threw myself onto my bed. I was absolutely devastated and within minutes, I was sobbing. I really, really want to be on that team. I yelled at Mom to go away, when she came to check on me and told her – I'M NOT GOING TO SCHOOL!!!!

I stayed in my room all morning and I think I was crying most of the time. This is so important to me – I desperately want to be on that team with my friends. Horse riding is my all-time favorite thing to do, but now that I've discovered netball, I've found that I love it as well! And the thought of not being on that team makes me really upset.

When I eventually stopped crying, I looked up

and noticed the sign that I had on my wall – I am now on the representative netball team and I am so excited!!!

My first impulse was to rip it off and throw it in the bin, but something made me stop. Instead I sat at my desk, found a really large sheet of poster paper and re-made the sign. This time though, it's big and bold and really colourful. Then I put it on my wall where I'll see it every day.

Mom was really surprized when I showed her but pleased that I've decided to have a positive attitude. Miracles can happen – is what she said – as long as you believe!

I've decided I'm going to be in that team!

Without even realizing it, I've made goals happen in the past and I'm going to make this happen as well – no matter what!!

Friday 11 April

Nikita called me tonight and convinced me to go to her pony club on Sunday, for a trial. I'm still not sure if I want to leave my club because it's really well organized with heaps of equipment and great instructors. And although I don't have any close friends there, everyone is really nice. I think I'd feel guilty if I did swap clubs.

But Mom said I may as well go and try it out and this Sunday is perfect because I don't have anything else on.

And it'll be so much fun to spend the day at pony club with Nikita and Jaz – I'm really looking forward to that!!

Sunday 13 April

Today was so cool. Being at pony club with two special horsey friends is the best thing ever! We got to hang out around the stables, which are something that my pony club doesn't have. Spending time with the horses in their stables and chatting with the other girls made it feel just like the Saddle Club! Everyone is really friendly and they have great instructors there as well. Even my favorite jumping instructor, Jim Jamieson teaches there. He only goes to my pony club occasionally as a special guest, so it's wonderful to know that he'll be teaching there every time that pony club is on,

Nikita loaned me a spare uniform polo shirt to wear as well, so I really felt like I belonged! And the girls now keep begging me to officially swap.

Oh, this is such a hard decision. I'm not sure what I should do.

But the exciting news is that I'm invited to go on a horse riding camp at North Shore in two weeks' time. Apparently there's fantastic trails and we can even ride on the beach! That is going to be so awesome. I've always wanted to ride on the beach.

I can't wait!!

Monday 14 April

I cannot believe it!!! Actually, yes of course I can believe it, because I made it happen!

This morning just before I was leaving for school, the phone rang and once again, I happened to answer it. When I realized it was the representative netball coach, I instantly felt a big knot in my stomach.

Then the best thing ever happened!!

She told me that one of the girls who plays in the defence position, cannot commit to the season now and won't be playing. She said that I'm the only other person who is suitable and can play her position, then she asked if I'd still like to join the team.

Well…my answer of course, was - YES! YES! YES! YES!

I'm in the team and I'm so excited!!! I feel like it's a miracle! And Mom is absolutely amazed. She says that I really did make it happen and I think I did as well.

"If you believe it, you can achieve it!"

I think I'm going to make a new poster with that motto on it for my bedroom wall.

I found a notebook in my drawer and I labelled

it – BOOK OF MIRACLES. I'm going to write all my goals down and see how many I can achieve.

I wonder what else I can make happen?

BOOK OF MIRACLES

Sunday 20 April

I've just come back from what I thought was going to be the most awesome weekend ever.

We had the pony club camp on the North Shore. It all started out really well – I was allowed to have the day off school on Friday and Dad took Tara and I to the camp site to meet all the others. We got the horses settled into their stables and our tents set up. I was camping with Nikita and Jo and it was all so exciting. Mom and Dad had arranged to come for the day on Sunday with Nate. There was no point to any of them staying over, because they'd be among the very few who weren't riding.

Everything was going fine – we rode on some really fun trails on Friday and Saturday and I walked Tara up towards the beach as well. She had started to become a bit nervous and flighty though, so I didn't take her all the way. I thought maybe the sound of the surf was scaring her, so I decided to leave it go until the following day. We'd all planned to have a big beach ride together and I was hoping that by then she'd have settled down.

But this ended up not being the case – in fact, it was further from it than I ever could have imagined!!

As soon as we finished breakfast, we all tacked

up and headed down towards the beach. Then it seemed that the minute Tara's hooves hit the sand, she became completely hypo! There was a lot of wind, the waves were crashing down and absolutely everything seemed to make her jump. A horse cantered past her and she kind of took off so I had to pull her up and turn her in a tight circle to try and settle her. Cars were racing past and she was so frisky. Anything and everything seemed to startle her and make her jump and shy. It was really scary! At this stage she was sort of half trotting, half prancing. I could not do anything with her.

Other riders had already raced off, galloping up the beach towards the swimming area at the very end. I was so jealous and so upset. That's what I had always wanted to do - gallop my pony along the beach but to even attempt that would have been lethal - she would have just taken off out of control. One of the older girls could see how crazy she was behaving and told me to get off and walk her which I did. But she was impossible for me to manage. Jaz's Dad, Mike saw me struggling and offered to take over, which was so good of him. He tried to lead her but she was running crazy circles all around him. A car stopped next to us and the driver, Jaz's mom who had seen what was going on, offered to give me a lift which I gladly accepted. I was so worried about Tara but it was scary being near her.

Somehow, Mike eventually made it to the end of the beach and reached the swimming area, with Tara still by his side. He then tied her to a truck that belonged to one of the parents and I had to sit nearby to keep an eye on her. I was so upset!! I'd never been on the beach with a horse before and I'd always wanted to be. Everyone was swimming with their horses and it was such a perfect place to be with them – as long as they were well-behaved that is! There were lovely shallow sections as well as deeper parts that were so nice for swimming. Watching everyone in the water with their horses was devastating!!!

I wanted Mom and Dad with me but they weren't there. I just wanted to cry! Whatever they were doing at that point, they certainly weren't aware of what I was going through. They told me later that they thought I'd be having the most wonderful time and it wasn't until they actually rang Jo to check on where they could meet up with us that they found out what was going on with Tara.

Jaz let me have a quick ride on her horse in the water but I just went in the shallow area and didn't actually get to swim, so it really wasn't the same. Then everyone decided to head back. One after the other, the horses all galloped back down the beach, racing each other, with the riders all having the time of their lives. Thank goodness, Jaz's mom offered me another lift but that meant Mike was left with Tara and by this stage she had become worse than ever!

Then all of a sudden we saw a green 4 wheel drive tearing up the beach towards us. I realized that it was Mom, Dad and Nate, coming to the rescue! By that time, they'd found out what was happening and were desperately trying to get to Tara and I as quickly as possible.

Poor Dad was then given the job of leading Tara back to the campsite and it was probably still a few kilometres away. The whole trip back down that beach she was totally spooked! Her eyes were wild and she was constantly shaking her head, whinnying and pulling at the lead rope. It was so hard for him to control her – she just wanted to take off. And can you imagine a runaway horse on an open beach that has cars racing up and down it all day? Poor Dad! That trip back down the beach was an absolute nightmare for him!

Meanwhile, Mike hopped in the car with Mom and drove back - his foot down on the pedal all the way, weaving and dodging the waves. This was very lucky for Mom because the tide was coming in and there wasn't much hard sand left to drive on. Mom's never driven on the beach before so it would have been really scary if she'd had to do the drive herself. Nate and his friend, who had also come along, thought this was the best part of all. For them, racing the car along the beach in 4 wheel drive, trying to keep the momentum going so that they didn't get bogged in soft sand, was the highlight of their day. They were so excited about the wild ride and desperate to do more of that. But by that stage, Mom and Dad had had enough excitement to last them a lifetime, I think and certainly didn't want to know about going anywhere back near the beach. By the time they both managed to return to camp, they were pretty stressed out – that's for sure!

So much for a relaxing day at North Shore!!

Then we got the shock of our lives when Mike came over to Tara's stable to check on her. He happened to notice the hay that she was steadily munching on – the hay that I'd taken from the bales Dad had bought from the stockfeed store for me to feed her throughout the weekend - the hay that she'd been eating since we arrived.

This hay is full of oats!!! This type of hay can make horses hot and send them completely crazy! No wonder she's been behaving so badly!

The look of shock and disbelief on Mike's face as those words poured from his mouth, explained it all!

Obviously this is what had happened to Tara. We couldn't believe that her feed had caused such a huge problem and was a disaster waiting to happen. Apparently it was the only hay available when Dad went to get the supplies for camp last week, but of course, he had no idea of the effects it could have. He said that he had queried it with the sales person, but was told that it was completely fine.

What a lesson for us!!!

Such a stressful day for everyone and it came so close to being a real disaster. And the worst part is that it could have been completely avoided!

Apparently some horses thrive on this type of hay and it isn't a problem at all, but we'll never buy it again, that's for sure and definitely not for Tara!!

Right now I'm just glad to be home again, safe in my room. And I'm so glad that everyone is back safe and sound, including Tara.

Today really was one of those days that you'd rather forget!

One thing is for sure though, I've certainly learned how important it is for horses to get the right feed!

Sunday 27 April

Shelley and Millie are back!!! This is the best news! Shelley's mom rang last night to ask if it would be okay to bring Millie back to our place. She said that it just hasn't been the same for Shelley since she moved. I guess the owners of that property aren't like us. Shelley is like family when she comes here and it's all so comfortable for her. On top of that, there's usually someone for her to ride with. It's no good agisting somewhere where you're not happy and Shelley loves being at our place. I'm sure Millie does too!

Tara was really pleased as well. They were so cute when they saw each other in the paddock today. Tara's ears instantly went forward and she walked straight on over to Millie to say hello. We're going to keep the two of them in the big paddock together now and Tammy's horses in the small paddock.

Things always seem to work out for the best! And we also played at our first all-day rep netball carnival for the season today and came second in our division. It was awesome. Today was such a great day! And thank goodness for that, especially after last weekend's drama! I have so many trophies now though - I think I'll have to ask Dad to put up another shelf in my room. It's pretty cool!

Wednesday 30 April

Nikita and Jaz have finally convinced me to join their pony club. We even went to a committee meeting tonight and it was heaps of fun. They're held once a month at the local pub. We all have dinner then the girls just hang out while the parents have the meeting. I loved it! It's so much fun to do something like that on a week night.

And the pony club gymkhana will be held in June which is very exciting! I hope Tara and I do as well as at the last one where I won my age group. That would be awesome. And the best thing is, because our birthdays are spread throughout the year, Nikita, Jaz and I have actually all ended up in different age groups. And this means we won't have to compete against each other. This is really good – we're definitely very close friends but we're still quite competitive.

I'm really looking forward to the gymkhana. I think I'd better fit in as much riding practice as possible before then, to make sure Tara is ready for it!

Sunday 4 May

Today was officially my first day of being a member at Jaz and Nikita's pony club! And we've managed to get our recipe book printed, so we're selling copies at the canteen. Already, we've sold 5, so that's a pretty good start. We should be able to sell heaps more at the gymkhana as well.

I worked on rider class today as well as my jumping and all the sporting events. Jim Jamieson was there again, which was really helpful. Especially because Tara has been pig rooting a lot! She even does it when we're about to go over a jump. I'm not as scared as I used to be and I try to be really firm with her, but it's definitely no fun, that's for sure.

Jim says that she's probably in season and it's pretty common for a mare's temperament to change at this time. He explained to me that they can become quite twitchy and sensitive, sometimes even unrideable. This is all because they're actually experiencing pain and will be quite grumpy. It's good to understand her behavior better, but it still doesn't make riding her any more enjoyable when she's like this. I hope she gets over it soon and especially before the gymkhana!s

Wednesday 17 May

Millie is really sick!

The vet has been here twice today to check on her. She has a terrible condition called laminitis. Shelley thinks that Millie's had it for a long time, as she often goes lame. The vet said that he agrees it's probably the cause of all the problems that Shelley has had with her.

They've treated the symptoms so many times before, but just when they think she's healing, it comes back. Shelley even took Millie to stay with a top equine vet on the outskirts of the city, as she'd heard that he's had success treating horses with this condition.

After keeping Millie for a couple of weeks and charging a heap of money, he just wanted to put her down. But there was no way Shelley was going to let that happen – especially on a stranger's property.

I'm so glad that Millie's back at our place. Shelley probably knew that this is where she would be happiest.

It's such a terrible problem for horses though. I've done some research on the internet about it and apparently one in every three horses and over 80% of ponies are in danger of laminitis right now! That is so bad!!!

And it sounds extremely painful! The hooves become badly inflamed inside which is what causes horses to become lame. I read that it's just like wearing out the soles of your shoes and having no protection on your feet whatsoever. And to add severe swelling to that would be terrible!

Shelley is in such a bad state. She does not know what to do. I think she has to decide whether to have Millie put down or not.

What a horrible situation to be in! Ali, next door, had to have her horse put down a while back after a snake bite. That's two chronically ill horses right here in our own little horsey world.

I didn't know what to say to Shelley when she left tonight.

It's so sad!!!

Friday 19 May

Millie was put down today.

It was the saddest thing!

Shelley was sobbing when she came back from the paddock. She had gone over there to say goodbye to her baby. I was watching her secretly, from the deck of our house when I got home from school this afternoon. I saw her mom put her arms around her and Shelley just sobbed and sobbed.

It was so awful!

Shelley's parents had arranged for an excavator to come and dig a pit to bury Millie in. Imagine seeing a big hole in the ground where your baby is going to be buried! I don't even want to think about it.

But at least, Millie is here on our property, which I think is very special. Shelley can visit her any time she wants and Millie will still be near Tara.

Shelley's parents said that they've had enough of horses – they've had lots of problems over the years (a bit like us I guess) and say that's the end of it all for Shelley.

But knowing Shelley, I think she'll have another horse before too long.

Wednesday 28 May

I still feel so sad about Millie.

I think of her every time I go to the paddock to ride. But it's lovely to think that her final resting place is in our paddock where we've all had so much fun together.

Poor Shelley! I haven't spoken to her since Millie died. It's really hard to know what to say. I feel bad talking about horses in front of her. I wonder if she'll end up getting a new pony. I hope so. It would be such a shame for her to give up riding – she loves it so much!

I've been riding Tara quite a bit lately, trying to get her fit and ready for the gymkhana. Thank goodness she's settled down a lot. I guess she's out of season now, but she can still be a handful and hard to control sometimes. I swear she wasn't like this when we first got her. She was so sweet and lovely back then. I remember Nate, who is an absolute beginner rider, was able to safely ride her without even being led and he also even managed to jump her, no problem whatsoever. Nothing seemed to bother her – she was so quiet and well-behaved! Maybe it's our grass or something? We do have mostly seteria – we make sure the heads of it are slashed, so none of the horses eat that part. But I wonder if the actual grass does have an effect.

Nikita's mom, Jo is an animal naturopath and we've often bought products from her to successfully treat problems in our horses and pets. Anyway, she thinks that the grass definitely has an impact on not only a horse's physical condition but also their temperament. She has actually had trouble with the horses at her place and it so happens that she has seteria there too. So she's trialled moving them to another property with better grass and amazingly enough, the horses have recovered from the condition they were in. So we wonder if that might have something to do with Tara's behavior! Maybe she's cranky because she's sore in places – possibly in her joints because of the grass she's been eating?

We've asked vets about it and they say that seteria is fine as long as the horses don't eat the heads off the top. But how can they be so sure?

I wish we knew the answer!

Saturday 31 May

Jaz and I went to Nikita's house today to see the new additions to her family. They now have 2 miniature ponies and they're the cutest things ever!! They are so gorgeous – I couldn't stop patting them! And they seem to have such a nice nature as well. Although we can see, that one is definitely the boss of the other. There's always that pecking order I guess, no matter what size horses are.

It's funny though, because we were at a property the other week where there was a miniature pony and an 18 hand draught horse. That horse was huge! It was so hilarious though, seeing the 2 of them together in the paddock – a giant next to a little baby. And it was really interesting to see that the huge horse was actually really gentle and wouldn't hurt a fly compared to the miniature that was the bossiest little pony I've ever seen! He certainly was in charge in that paddock!

Sunday 1 June

We had another rep netball carnival today. Out of the 6 games we played, we won 4, tied one and lost one. So we did really well.

I absolutely love netball. I'm so glad that Mom convinced me to play!

And next weekend, we're all going away for the weekend to a state carnival. The whole team is staying in a motel. It's going to be awesome!!

Mom is coming too, so Dad will have to look after Tara while I'm away. But he told me today, that even though I'm playing netball, I still have to focus on riding and give Tara the attention she deserves. I know he's right, and I will, but I'm really enjoying netball. It's so much fun playing a team sport with a heap of really nice girls!

Tuesday 10 June

Oh my gosh, I've just come back from the best weekend ever!!!!!

We actually got back last night and I did not want to go to school today, I was so tired!! We played heaps of games over the 3 days – yesterday was a public holiday so we got to have 3 full days of netball. I'm already looking forward to next year's state carnival because I don't think I've ever had so much fun in my entire life!

Staying in a motel with the whole team, having all our meals together and playing so much netball was absolutely awesome!!! We ended up coming third in our division and even got a medal. Our coach was so pleased with us – we all played really well.

But the weekend was freeeeeeezing!!!! Apparently the town where we played is famous for being really, really cold, but we didn't expect it to be that cold! There was even sleet falling on Sunday morning when we got out of the bus and we actually had to take our tracksuits off so that we could play. I don't think I've ever felt so cold! I'm really glad that the temperature never gets that low where we live!!

And the local shops actually sold out of beanies and woollen scarves! Hundreds of girls were in town for the weekend, to play netball in the state carnival and we heard that the shops were completely cleaned out of all their warm clothing.

At least we had our team tracksuits to wear and I'd taken a really warm pink beanie and scarf as well. I'm so pleased I did and they were perfect because they not only kept me warm but they matched our uniform perfectly!

Even though it was freezing cold, none of us really cared – we were all having too much fun!

I really do think it was the best weekend I've ever had!!

Sunday 15 June

I am so upset! I've seen some terrible things happen with the horses, but today was the worst!

We had the gymkhana and it all started off being heaps of fun. Although Tara was mucking up a bit, I still managed to win ribbons in lots of the events that I went in and Nikita and Jaz also did really well.

We sold a heap of our home-made horsey treats and several copies of our recipe book to riders from other clubs. We were so happy! We were even talking about having to print more copies as there were only a few left.

Then it was time to start the afternoon programme. I went to bounce pony, Jaz had rider class and Nikita went to her jumping event.

I remember looking down the hill after I'd had my turn going over the bounce pony logs and I saw Nikita on Latte, cantering up the slope. She'd just finished the final jump of her round then all of a sudden, almost in the blink of an eye, she was in the air. Latte had literally bucked her off and I watched in horror as she went flying over his head! At that moment, my heart seemed to stop. I saw her land flat on her back on the ground in front of him and it was then, I think that I screamed – Nikita!!!!

I've witnessed some scary things since I've had a horse, but this is at the top of the list! To see my best friend thrown off her horse like that and then lying deathly still on the ground, was terrifying!

I raced Tara out of the bounce pony ring and headed down towards where Nikita lay. By this time she was surrounded by adults and I could not see what was going on. Jaz appeared at my side – she'd seen it happen as well – and we both started to cry.

One of the adults was calling an ambulance but we just wanted to know if Nikita was okay! How badly hurt was she??? Was she conscious?? And worse still, had she been crippled or even killed??? We just wanted to know!! All we could see was the lower half of her body but she wasn't moving.

I'll never forget those minutes while we waited for the ambulance to arrive. It seemed absolutely endless!

As I think back over what happened today, sitting here in my bedroom, surrounded by photo frames with pictures of me and my two best friends, laughing and having so much fun together, it doesn't seem that it could possibly be real. If only it could simply be a very bad dream!

But it's not, it did happen. I was there to see the whole thing and now poor Nikita is lying strapped to a hospital bed with suspected spinal injuries and that's all we know. That's all they could tell us when we rang.

I feel so unbelievably upset right now. I can't bear to think of her in that condition.

It's really, really hard, but I just have to picture her in my mind being absolutely fine - walking again, right by my side, laughing and happy – the way she always is.

She has to be okay, she just has to!!!!!!!!!!!!!!!!

Nikki and Latte at pony club…

Everything was going so well!!

Monday 14 June

We've just arrived back home from visiting Nikita in the hospital. I was worried sick all day at school today. I couldn't concentrate on anything! I was just desperate to visit her and see that she was okay.

As soon as visiting hours started this afternoon, we were at that hospital door – Mom, Dad and I went to visit and it broke my heart to see her lying so helpless in that hospital bed.

Thank goodness, she hasn't been crippled – but she has fractured her spine in 2 places. They said that she is a very, very lucky girl. If it had been even slightly worse, she may never have been able to walk again. She'll be in hospital for a couple of weeks I think, then when she comes home, she has to wear a special supportive brace for about 2 months. It was such a huge relief to also hear that she will eventually still be able to ride, although jumping will definitely be out of the question.

Nikita's parents were there with her and her mom, Jo was an emotional mess. She said that it was so hard to see Nikita lying there in all that pain and when Jo started crying, I couldn't help but cry as well.

I don't think she'll even be up to eating the chocolates that I took her and chocolate is her all-time favorite! But hopefully the bunch of flowers we brought will help to cheer her up just a little bit.

I feel really sad thinking of her there but I'm so relieved that she's going to be alright.

Wednesday 15 June

We went to visit Nikita again and already she seems to have improved. It hurts her a lot whenever she has to move and it must be really hard for her laying still on her back 24 hours a day. But I was pleased to see that she's already had some of the chocolates that we brought her the other night – I knew she wouldn't be able to resist.

We talked about what happened on Sunday and Nikita said that she doesn't really remember the accident. She has a clear picture of finishing the event and thought that she had even won it. She then asked her mom if she had collected her winning ribbon. That was definitely a good sign. There she was lying in a hospital bed with a badly fractured spine and all she was worried about was the ribbon that she had won in the gymkhana!

After cantering up the slope, though, she has no recollection of what happened next. She only remembers waking up on the ground surrounded by people and wondering how on earth she had got there.

It's probably a good thing that she doesn't remember it – it would not be a nice memory to have!

Anyway, I'm going back to visit her on the

weekend and the great news is, that she may even be able to go home early next week. This is such a good thing – she hates hospital food and being a vegetarian, it's hard to get a decent meal. So her parents have been bringing her meals from home and also getting some dishes from the restaurant down the road. Luckily, they do good vegetarian meals there!

I think I'll take her some more chocolates when I go back on Saturday. She'll really like that!

Sunday 26 June

I went to pony club today but it wasn't the same without Nikita. And Jaz wasn't able to go today either, so I didn't really enjoy it very much.

I think Tara is back in season – she was pigrooting again – not a lot but enough to be annoying. I really wish she wouldn't do that!

And now we've been told that pony club is only going to meet once a month. For some reason, their member numbers are down and having to pay for instructors is expensive. So I guess they can't really afford to hold it more often.

My old pony club meets every 2 weeks and has heaps of members. I wonder how they're all going. It really is a great club and has so much to offer. I'm starting to wonder if I should have changed clubs after all.

At least I have netball with all my team mates – so that's something to look forward to.

But the best news is that Nikita came home during the week. She now has to wear a special brace which was made specifically to fit her body. It has to be worn all day, every day, under her clothes. Lucky it's winter now, so the weather is cooler which will make it more bearable to wear.

I visited her yesterday, after my netball game and she was so happy to see me. She's very bored though, the poor thing – all she can do is lay in bed or lay flat on the lounge. She's in quite a bit of pain when she moves as well, so she has to stay as still as possible.

I went to pat the minis before I left. They really are the cutest. I could see Latte grazing in the bottom paddock. I'm sure he misses Nikita too. Jo said that she's going to get a trainer and healer for him as well as a saddle fitter as soon as Nikita's better. She wants to check any possibilities for why he behaved that way because he's never done anything like that before.

Jo thinks he has a sore back which made him buck – and if he does, that definitely explains his behavior. If I had a sore back, I wouldn't want anyone riding me either. He may have been in heaps of pain and couldn't stand it anymore so he just wanted to get Nikita off. Anyway, the paddock rest will do him good. I suggested that Jo try calling Dieter, the Swiss trainer and animal acupuncturist. He was brilliant in helping me with Tara's problem, so I'm sure he can help Latte too.

I really hope he can!

Saturday 2 August

We won again at netball today. Our team is doing really well and we'll probably make the finals. There's another carnival for the rep team tomorrow as well. So I'm not going to get a chance to ride at all this weekend. I actually haven't ridden for a few weeks!! There's been extra netball training sessions on and I've been busy with homework. I've also just realized that I forgot it was Tara's official birthday yesterday. How could I have forgotten that? I'm going to have to make it up to her!

Mom and Dad have commented that I haven't done much riding lately, but to be honest, I haven't really wanted to. I do ride occasionally, but Shelley doesn't have Millie anymore so I can't ride with her. Nikita is obviously out of action and that will probably be until the end of the year and Jaz has been busy every time I'm free. So we haven't had a chance to get together at all. As for Cammie and Grace, they've actually moved their horses to an equestrian type place just nearby. They've said that it has the most beautiful arena to ride in and their horses also get stabled, rather than just being in the paddock.

So that just leaves Ali, but she's older now and off socializing with her friends, I guess. I don't think she does much riding either.

Also, to be honest, Tara has been a bit of a handful lately. It's probably because I'm not riding her enough, but when I do ride, it isn't that much fun.

I don't know what I'm going to do. I think I really should have stayed at my own pony club. At least that way, I'd have the pony club days to look forward to each fortnight. My new pony club is meeting again next Sunday, but I have another netball carnival on. There's so many of them, and we love them – they're so much fun!!

But this means, I'm going to have wait 5 weeks until pony club is next on. That's so long to wait!! I hope Jaz goes at least, otherwise it won't be much fun at all!!

Sunday 7 September

We had our last netball carnival for the season today. We ended up winning as well – it was such a great way to end the season! But I'm going to miss it so much. I'll have to find room somewhere to put my trophy – my shelves are full of them. I've even put my ribbons from horse riding up everywhere and my room looks so cool now!

Speaking of riding, I've hardly ridden at all for the last month. Pony club was on today but I couldn't go because of the netball carnival. Dad told me tonight that if I don't ride then he's selling Tara. I told him that the main reason is her behavior – which is true really – she was so sweet and gentle when we first bought her, even Nate was able to hop on her and go over jumps, for goodness sake. There is no way in the world that he could do that on her now – it would be too dangerous. She'd just take off.

Mom and Dad have suggested that if we do sell her, we could then look for a horse with a quieter nature, although take our time and definitely not rush into it. Nikita and I look at horses online all the time. There's so many lovely ponies for sale. But I'm too attached to her, to think about selling her - even though I hardly ride. I don't think I could do it!

Also, I'm wondering if Mom and Dad really would get me another horse if Tara goes. Maybe they're just saying that. I know that she's definitely going to waste though and needs to be ridden. She is still such a beautiful horse and I love her to death regardless of her behavior!

I don't know what to do!!

Friday 19 September

Mom and Dad told me tonight that they've actually found someone who is really keen to buy Tara! They decided a couple of weeks ago to advertise her online and just see what response they get, then take it from there.

Well of course, she would be snapped up – she's so beautiful and she really is a great all-rounder. But I can't believe that they're really talking about selling her. I knew that it might happen but now it looks like it's actually for real.

The lady is from interstate – apparently she's always wanted an Arab and thinks Tara looks gorgeous, which of course, she does. Dad told her all about Tara 's history and how she hasn't been ridden much lately. He also told her that she's been misbehaving as well. But can you believe it, she's not worried about that at all! Dad also asked what type of grass she has on her property and thank goodness, it's not seteria. Dad's hoping that will really make a difference.

The lady – her name's actually Amanda - has just moved to a rural property and is very keen to get horses for herself and her daughter. She said that they'll both probably do pony club and as well, she'd like to do endurance riding. I know Tara would love that – the more she's ridden, the better behaved she is.

But we can't believe that Amanda actually wants to buy her sight unseen! She says that Tara is just what she's been looking for and knows that she's the horse for her. Mom said that she does sound really nice and I'm sure she is, but it's such a big thing to do! Apparently, she's even agreed to buy my stuben saddle. Dad told her this was bought especially for Tara and is what must be used when riding her which Amanda said she's more than happy to do. She said that she just wants to do the right thing by Tara.

I guess if Tara is going to be sold, that she does sound like the perfect new owner. But it still doesn't make it any easier for me. And the other issue is that Tara will have to travel overnight on a truck – which is a huge trip for her! But Mom said that Amanda's looked into transport companies and found one that is highly recommended. Mom rang to check up on them and they make regular stops on the way to feed and water the horses and also to exercise them. They also stop to stay overnight at a horse property with stables where the horses get some time in a paddock to feed and exercise as well.

So it does all sound really good and Mom and Dad have promised me that after she's gone, we can look out for another horse.

But, I feel really sad at the thought of selling my baby – she really was my dream pony and I thought I'd have her for many years to come.

This is such a big decision!

Deep down, I know that Mom and Dad are right though. Tara deserves better – she deserves to be ridden and is too nice a horse to go to waste in the paddock. It really isn't fair on her.

Mom and Dad are saying it's the best thing for her and I think they've actually pretty much told Amanda that we will be happy for her to take Tara. And apparently there is a transport truck with an available place leaving next week.

But that's only a week away! 1 more week and then she'll be gone! I really can't believe this has happened so quickly!!

I did not expect this to happen.

I thought I'd have Tara forever!

I'm going to miss her so much!!

Thursday 25 September

As soon as I got home from school, I got changed, grabbed my grooming kit and Tara's favorite horsey treats that I made last night then headed on over to the paddock to give her a bath. I wanted to make sure she looks beautiful for her new owner.

I knew it would be my last chance to spend time with her and she just loves being brushed, so after bathing her, that's what I did. I combed her mane and tail and talked to her the whole time.

She gobbled up the treats I'd made and licked her lips the way she always does. I put her rug on to keep her warm overnight as well as to stay nice and clean for the trip. I then gave her a huge hug, added some extra feed to her bucket and came back down to the house.

I really don't know how I'm going to say goodbye tomorrow!

And I don't think I'll be able to sleep tonight.

I can't stop thinking about my baby and all the wonderful times we've had together.

I know there's been lots of near disasters, especially this year – but they're not the memories that stand out in my mind!

I remember the day that I first saw her. I just

knew that she was the pony for me. We've had so many special times together. I'll always remember the fun we've had – so many gymkhanas and so many competitions – all the trophies and ribbons, all those days spent at pony club and the absolutely amazing pony club camp with Nikita and Jaz last year – that was so much fun – I'll never forget that!

I'm so lucky to have had Tara and experience all these wonderful things.

I think I'll dream about her tonight – maybe we'll compete in a gymkhana together – clear all the jumps and finish first in the ideal time then win a blue ribbon. That would be such a nice dream to have!

I love you Tara!

Friday 26 September

Dad picked me up from school early today then we went home and loaded Tara onto the float. We had about an hour's drive to take her to the pickup point of the trucking company for her journey interstate.

I'd packed some more treats for her for the trip, as well as a few buckets of her favorite feed. They'll feed her grass hay along the way, but we want to make sure she has her regular feed, or it could really affect her. We now know the issues that can come about when you suddenly change a horse's diet and it would be terrible for something bad to happen on the way - all because she'd eaten the wrong food.

We had about 15 minutes with her before she had to go. I gave her a huge hug and some more treats and told her that I love her. As I patted her gently, I whispered in her ear – I love you Tara! I told her how sorry I am not to be keeping her. I also told her that I'd be ringing her new owner every week to check that she's doing okay. I had a huge knot in the pit of my stomach and couldn't stop the tears that started to fall. When the driver took her from me, I suddenly felt like I was losing my best friend.

I think that moment was one of the saddest I've ever experienced! And right now, in in my room, surrounded by photos of my two darling ponies, along with all the ribbons and trophies that we've won together, all I want to do is cry.

This afternoon, as she was walking calmly and willingly onto the truck, I thought to myself – What have I done??? – Have I made a huge mistake???

As I watched her drive way, I had the sinking feeling that I may never own a horse as beautiful again!

Goodbye Tara…

I will never forget you!!!

Afterword...

The day that I loaded Tara onto the transport truck so that she could travel interstate to her new home was my saddest day ever! The trip home with Dad was very quiet and he tried to cheer me up by stopping at our favorite ice creamery to buy me a huge tropical ice cream sundae – my absolute favorite. But nothing would work. I felt devastated that I had actually sold my dream pony, even though there'd been so many problems and she had become quite difficult to handle.

I spent the next few months, looking on various websites for a new horse – a really good all-rounder with a lovely nature. There were so many beautiful horses for sale, but it was hard to find exactly what I was looking for.

Mom and Dad weren't keen to rush into anything and we decided to take our time. Meanwhile, I continued to play netball and absolutely loved the time I spent with my team mates, playing, competing and having loads of fun together.

As the months went by, I found that with all the demands of school work, playing netball and being busy with friends, life was a lot easier without a horse.

In hindsight, I realize that I should have stayed

with my original pony club, which really was absolutely fabulous and I would probably still be riding now if that had been the case. So I have certainly learned a lesson from that!

Even though none of us ride horses anymore, Nikita and Jaz are still two of my closest friends and I know that we will definitely be friends forever!

I still love horses and I always will!!! Maybe I'll have a horse mad daughter myself one day and will experience the wonderful world of horses all over again.

***

***

Thank you for reading Diary of a Horse Mad Girl.

If you enjoyed it, I would be very grateful if you would leave a review on Amazon.

Your support really does make a difference!

Thank you so much!

Katrina ☺

Please Like our Diary of a Horse Mad Girl Facebook page

- *A fabulous page for all horse loving girls…*

DiaryofaHorseMadGirl

And be sure to follow us on Instagram

@juliajonesdiary

@freebooksforkids

Have you read the Julia Jones' Diary series yet?

Julia Jones' Diary books can be purchased individually or as a collection at a DISCOUNTED PRICE!

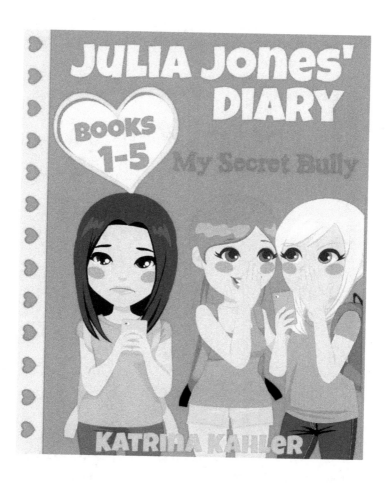

Julia Jones' Diary: My Dream Pony

This is a collection that combines two wonderful books for all horse loving girls. These books can be read alone and do not have to be read as part of the Julia Jones' Diary series.

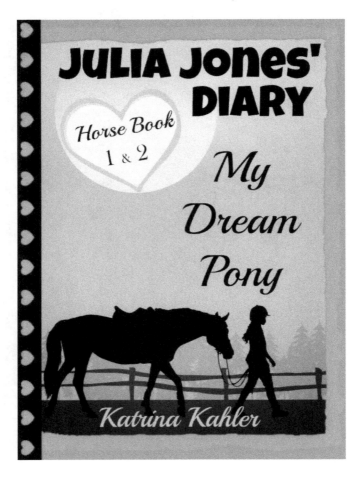

CPSIA information can be obtained
at www.ICGtesting.com
Printed in the USA
BVHW041857041218
534777BV00009B/344/P